Th

About

A brutal murder. Mysterious markings carved into the victim. A forgotten prophecy. A reactivated, long-lost robot. A stripping cow. A ruthless politician. A conspiracy which threatens to bring Paradise to its knees.

Paradise, 2301: 200 years ago, following WWIII, the utopian Paradise formed from the remnants of the European Alliance. Since then, its citizens - the Great Nine - live peacefully and harmonically on European soil. The only surviving bastion following the Great War, Paradise has become a place where the arts and generosity flow freely among cows and eagles, horses and donkeys, apes and foxes, cats and dogs, humans and robots. Until the brutal murder of a bull shakes Paradise to its core. Who murdered him? Why? And what do the markings carved into the victim mean?

To investigate, the long-deactivated and fully restored robot Helmut is brought back to life. His mission: identify the murderer and bring them to the ruthless and power-hungry Cow Councillor Christine. But can she be trusted? On which side is she? What sides are there? Helmut soon realises things aren't what they seem to be and he finds himself entangled in a silent war, a vast conspiracy, which threatens to bring Paradise to its knees. As if things weren't absurd enough already, Helmut encounters the stripping cow Marguerite. It is love at first sight.

The Glitch

The Paradise Chronicle

Book One

Tim Cers

First Edition

Contact Information:
timcers.com

Disclaimer:

The characters in this book are entirely fictional. Any resemblance to actual persons living or dead is entirely coincidental. Any references to real places or historical events are used fictitiously and their place in the novel are the product of the author's imagination.

To my parents,
whose empathy and love guided me,
and who taught me to be myself.

To my sister,
who loves me unconditionally,
despite my flaws.

To my grandparents,
who enabled me to read from an early age,
and sparked my imagination.

Acknowledgments

To…

… Felix. Without you, this story wouldn't exist. I never imagined nursing a hangover on a French farm would inspire me to write any story, let alone this one.

… Luca & Anja, Sigmund & Kim. You've become my second family. I love you dearly.

… my draft readers. Without you, this novel wouldn't have become what it is today. Thank you for your patience, your criticism, and the occasional bottle of wine.

… Savina, who got me in touch with my editor, Morelle. Without you, this book wouldn't be the same. Thank you both for your edits, your encouragement, and enlightened comments.

… Charlotte C. Not only are you a great artist, but also a magnificent friend. Without you, I would have been lost more often than not.

Part I - The Rise of the Robot

Prologue

The Creation

The bright sun stood high in the sky, embracing the celebrating crowd with warm rays. Thousands and thousands of creatures attended today's celebration; humans walked side by side with robots, cows and bulls jogged underneath the broad wings of majestic eagles, nimble cats jumped alongside dogs, apes walked upright, donkeys flirted with horses, and the birds sang of the glorious times, of the here and now. Even a few foxes could be spotted among the ever-growing crowd. Huge dark blue banners showing a mighty white tree hung from bright buildings, fluttering in the wind like the long blonde hair of innocent children. Today marked the 200th anniversary of the Creation of Paradise. Some of today's crowd had been present when the Accord had been signed, but most who attended today's celebrations had not seen the light of day for decades to come when the Survivors had come together to found the world as they knew it today. The crowd walked by the statues of the founding members. Tall and shiny they stood around the City's main square, reminding everyone of the good times they enjoyed. The crowd cheered every time they passed another of the five statues. It was a meaningful day, and festive it was, indeed.

Not far away from the procession, and yet high above it, a lonely bull ran for his life. Faster than Franculo had ever gone, he adopted a horse's gallop to escape the inevitable. His four hooves were desperately moving faster than ever before. If only he could make his way to the procession, he could warn them of what was to come. Deep down, he knew that he couldn't make it, but he would try nonetheless for those who didn't attempt the impossible would never reach the stars. Franculo felt blood pouring out of the wound on his flank, felt the pain and coldness that came with such wounds slowly setting in. His pursuer wouldn't be far behind and didn't leave him any room for mistakes. A quick look over his shoulder confirmed his hunch. They were right behind him now, and he had nowhere to go. Abruptly, he stopped before a high glass window which he had almost overlooked. Hundreds of meters underneath him, he saw the procession flow towards the City's main square like water running through a riverbed. His eyes jumped from right to left, back to centre where his pursuer now entered the big hall, a wide grin on the lips. Despite the vastness of the hall, and the procession in the streets, he heard nothing but his blood slowly dropping on the dark floor - popp. Franculo took a deep breath and looked in the happily cruel eyes of his pursuer. There was no escaping the inevitable. Popp. Popp. Popp!

Loud, cheerful music followed the procession. The beat of drums determined the speed of the crowd, which had slowly but surely found its way onto the City's main square, where the Council met the ever-growing procession. Just when the last of the many citizens had joined the march, the parade began. If the drums had been loud before, their rhythm seemed to speed up even more, and the sound of heralding glory poured over the procession. The crowd began to cheer loudly when the first of the parade entered the square. Large cavalry cows with mounted MGs on their backs mightily galloped through the lane opening for them. The cows' hooves mirrored the beat of the drums, their hide reflecting the blue and white colours of Paradise, their eyes prideful and electrifying. These were the descendants of the brave souls who had aided the long-lost Alliance during WWIII, saving it from the horrors of war and death. Cows and bulls had been given a place in Paradise for their courageous efforts to preserve peace in times of war.

For this bull, however, death was much closer than peace, no matter what side Franculo's ancestors had fought for. All that mattered was which side he was fighting for today. With a sweeping motion, his pursuer aimed at the fleeing bull and took another shot. Without a sound, the bullet catapulted towards its target, hitting the bull's rear left leg a fraction of a second after pulling the trigger. The bull cried out loud and collapsed just in front of one of the big windows from which he had been trying to escape. He felt the pain in his leg, felt how the blood left his body and how his eyelids became heavier. Slowly at first, but it took him more and more effort to keep them open. His body shook violently, and he felt the wet pool of blood forming around his body, touching his hide. Through the glass, he watched the procession underneath him, watched his brothers and sisters parade through the streets, unable to warn them. They had no idea the prophecy had begun. Only he knew. Franculo, and his pursuer, whom he heard approaching behind him. Gentle, soft steps which could only mean one thing.

Gigantic robots followed the cows. Their heavy steps shattered stones and overshadowed the drums, but not the cheer of the crowd when the first of them entered the square. Those were the upgraded infantry units which fought during the Last War. For today's procession, their armour had been remodelled, following the design during WWIII. These robots reminded everyone of what most had never lived through; that once upon a time, Europe had not been a paradise, but a bloody field of war, saved by the invention of fighting AI. These had been some of the most advanced mechanical lives yet, and under the guidance of human generals, they had aided the cows' cavalry in protecting the continent. Today, of course, people cheered for fighting robots were not needed anymore inside Paradise. Today, robots served alongside all other creatures in a peaceful, harmonious Paradise like the world had never seen before.

The bull couldn't move anymore. His body was too weak for anything really. Franculo felt coldness setting in, starting from his flank and leg, reaching all the way over to the other side of his body, where he lay in a wet pool of his own blood. Though his eyes were heavy, he still kept them open. His pursuer had reached him now and swiftly kneeled down beside him, holding a sharp knife. The bull cried out helplessly when the cold steel touched his hide, permeated his flesh, reaching the arteries underneath it. Franculo felt the ancient markings being carved on his body. Then, suddenly, from one moment to the next, the pain stopped, and the bull turned its head. He saw his pursuer standing upright, an almost apologetic smile on the lips. The bull's eyes wandered down to the gun. The safety catch was off and prepared to fire a bullet right between his eyes. The bull was almost relieved, and for a short moment, Franculo couldn't feel the pain anymore. He felt warmth embrace him, carry him away, towards the sky. His body had become a sanctuary - a sanctuary with ancient markings on it, nonetheless. In that short moment of peace, he realised what all this meant, what role they had quite literally carved out for him. Determination manifested in his eyes. He would die today, but at least he would die on his terms and disrupt his purser's plan. One last time, adrenaline pumped through Franculo's body, and he returned the smile with wicked eyes.

Then, just when the Council began to speak, glass shattered. Under usual circumstances, nobody would have heard it. The drums alone would have been enough to mask the sound of breaking glass. Even without the drums, the crowd would have cheered, and everyone would have missed it. Even if the drums had not been playing and the crowd had been silent, the loud voice of the Council would have overshadowed the shattering glass. But not this time. The glass broke just when everyone was quiet, when the drums stopped playing, the crowd stopped cheering, but the Council hadn't begun to speak yet. So, when the glass shattered loudly, thousands and thousands of creatures on the City's square abruptly turned their heads to its origin high above them. Sharp human eyes recognised a massive falling object, and the even sharper eyes of the eagles recognised it for what it was; a falling bull. The robots recognised the shape of the bull, but couldn't make sense of it for a bull falling from a window wasn't a simulation that had been installed on their systems. The cows' eyesight, by no means terrible, couldn't quite match that of humans and eagles, so all they recognised was a falling object. Huge apes gasped aloud, donkeys stopped flirting with horses for just a second, cats and dogs screamed in despair. Then, the falling bull crashed onto the square, exploding in a fountain of blood and bones, brain and cells, his four legs scattered around the City's square. For the first time in 200 years, blood was shed in Paradise.

Chapter One

The Awakening

Creatures who played god never succeeded; not if she had a say in it. The metallic, hollow sound of long-dead machinery welcomed Christine in the dark hangar. The cow's eyes slowly wandered through the hall. Dust lay thickly on the floor, and the doors were rusty and brownish. It seemed like nobody had come here in decades which was probably still even too generous. Two bodyguard cows followed Christine into the hangar. Their four hooves barely made any sound despite the light MGs mounted on their backs. The dust silenced their every step, deluding anyone who could have been in the hangar of their presence. But of course, the hall hadn't seen a living soul in decades. With a sudden clicking noise, the massive light bulbs turned on. What once would have filled the hangar with vivid light now only provided dim illumination. Barely enough to see throughout the enormous hall. No light from the outside entered the hangar, no sunshine had ever touched its bricks and machinery. Christine majestically glided through the dust. Walking over it as if it was water. Her hooves made no sound at all. The bodyguards' eyes flickered from one corner to the other and ultimately rested on the robot walking in front of them.

"Has anyone been here since the deactivation?"

"No, Councillor Christine", the service robot replied with a metallic sound.

An older model then, Christine figured. It didn't surprise her that the Council hadn't stationed more superior models here. To them, this hangar was just one of many. To her, it was the door to the promised land.

"What happened here? That was a little before my time, pardon me. The records are somewhat ominous on this establishment."

"No need to apologise, Councillor. Almost nobody knows about this. It is highly classified, and it isn't part of the public record. I might be the only service robot to have been upgraded with this knowledge given my placement. Anyone trying to enter this facility without permission would have been instantly frozen. This is the home of the last Combrine. Robot 941120 was the newest model of the now-vanished Timcorps Enterprises, an early robot and software manufacturer, among other things. Robot 941120 was part of the Combrine-series. A promising, powerful creation of advanced AI and self-thinking robots, which were supposed to be able to guard our borders while having some sort of EQ which made them sensitive enough to understand human emotion, though not to experience it themselves. They would have been the smartest AI yet, equipped with the newest technology. The series promised to revolutionise the way Paradise would have functioned and was ultimately designed to combine the best of both humanity and robots. It was meant as a continuous step towards humanising robots and providing them with a life worth living as was promised by the First Councillor Emilia, the Great. A gentle thought by our creators. Sensitive AI though was too good to be true. After all Council tests were passed, the First Combrine Regiment was sent to Sig's Canal for a trial run in real life. During their first mission, they encountered a militarised band of humans who tried to cross the Canal. After a short battle, these wildlings surrendered. As was practised back then, the regiment was ordered to execute all prisoners on the spot. Robot 941120 refused the order. Upon return to their base, he claimed that it was unjust to execute unarmed creatures and that he would not oblige to such orders. He was immediately switched off, his memory wiped and software destroyed."

The service robot stopped for a second and looked at Christine who seemed fascinated by the idea. Her tail was excitedly wagging through the air.

"That was a long time ago. Years have passed since then. Generations have been born and died. The world is a different place now."

They had stopped in front of another old door. This

one was even thicker than the original entrance to the hangar. The service robot opened the door with a sweeping motion of its metallic hand. Everything the robot did seemed so effortless.

"He doesn't look like a robot", the Councillor exclaimed breathlessly.

Of course, she had read about their human-like appearance, but she had never actually seen one of them before. Almost no living creature had for all she knew. It had been Timcorps Enterprises' last action to destroy all evidence of their doomed creation.

"That was the brilliance of the Combrine-series. You wouldn't have known that they weren't human. They would have looked, acted and experienced their surroundings just like real humans. Even their outer layers were made of hybrid skin to keep the illusion alive. Some say they even bleed real blood, but that's probably just a legend. Nobody would have known the difference. They were the ultimate promise."

"Why was the entire series discontinued then? They seem… useful."

Christine continued to stare at the robot. It wasn't just that he looked like a human, he looked just like him. The cheekbones, the way the eyebrows were plucked, the somewhat careless haircut, the way the shoulders straightened without moving. Her eyes wandered down the robot's body and absorbed every detail about him.

"The risk was too big. Nobody ever figured out why Robot 941120 malfunctioned the way he did. The premature destruction of his being made sure of that. Even if it was just the one robot that malfunctioned, who knew whether he would remain the only one. Nobody foresaw that the creations could be more humanised than their creators. They even gave each other names. Randomly assembled names, that is."

"Oh, really. What was this one called?"

"We can't be certain, Councillor. They kept them to themselves. But for all we know, it could have been either Naker, Tumleh, Nussa, or Elmilech."

"Interesting. What happened then?"

"The Council ordered all of them to return to their home to figure out what happened. Back to this hangar. None returned, however. On their way back, they were caught in a huge fire on the Titanic III. Only Robot 941120 survived on account of being shipped through a different route after its deactivation. Upon his arrival, First Councillor Thommy ordered his continuous de-activation and storage in this facility. Since then, not a living soul has come close to him. Except me, of course."

"We're nature's audacity," the Councillor whispered quietly.

It was silent then. The disturbed dust had come to rest on the floor again, almost covering the cows' tracks like freshly fallen snow. Christine looked at the deactivated robot as if she was waiting for a response, shifting her weight to her front hooves, her entire body expectantly leaning forward. But the sleeping robot didn't respond, not a word left his lips, nothing suggested that he was still alive. For a moment it seemed as if the Councillor would be disappointed, but then a smile began to cover her face.

"Pardon me, my lady. May I ask a question?"

One of the bodyguard cows stepped forward. If the Councillor was surprised, she didn't show it.

His heavy steps resounded in the hangar despite the thick layer of dust all around the four creatures.

"Be my guest."

"Why did you list those four names specifically, Service? Why are only they known?"

"Excellent question, Sir. When they accounted for the robots on the Titanic III, all robot IDs, their calling sign so to speak, were present, but three nicknames weren't added to the attendance list signed by the robots themselves. Legend has it that three of his compatriots went missing during their original mission and have since been living right under our noses."

"Really?", Christine gasped and rapidly distanced herself from the robot.

The service robot grinned artificially.

"That was a joke, Councillor. My apologies. My

creators are currently attempting to teach robots humour. Apparently, they haven't quite figured it out yet. Maybe with the next service update. I heard it's gonna be a big one. The one thing us robots cannot consistently do is use and understand sarcasm."

The Councillor laughed.

"Don't worry, Service. I'm sure your kind will learn that skill eventually."

"Thank you, Councillor."

Christine took a deep breath and exhaled through her lips. Memories flashed in front of her eyes and she seemed to stare into the nothingness of long forgotten days.

Her eyes narrowed a bit and she took a step towards the deactivated robot. It was time. She lifted her left hoof and pressed the red button next to the hollow robot fixed in his cell. A second later, dark brown eyes opened suddenly.

Chapter Two

The Becoming

Dark, brown eyes opened suddenly, reflecting in Christine's crystal blue eyes. Magnificent.

"Robot 941120, this is your Commanding Officer Councillor Christine."

"I'm awaiting your orders, Councillor Christine."

The Councillor quickly jumped a step back and stared at the robot with wide eyes. Her four hooves simultaneously landed in the whirling dust. His voice was so gentle, so calm. So human and so very non-robotic. What a stark contrast to the metallic sound of the service robot. What a remarkable difference to anything she had encountered in recent years. She shook her head in quiet disbelief. He was magnificent. So pretty. And so familiar.

"Robot 941120, it's Commanding Officer Councillor Christine, not Councillor Christine. Now perform a manufacturer check."

"Your wish is my command, COCC."

The creature slowly stood up to perform all essential movements that were required to function. The robot almost lazily stretched his arms, then his legs, bent over and touched the ground before he cracked his neck. All of that and more he did in utter, sharp silence. The entire hangar was silent and seemed to focus purely on the movements of Robot 941120. Even the cow bodyguards followed the spectacle closely, fascinated by his movements, watched the human-like manifestation gently move through different poses almost as if he was performing yoga instructions, and forgot that they served to protect the Councillor. The newly awoken robot was smooth and sharp like an Olympic gymnast. Then, all of a sudden, the robot stopped moving entirely, and his eyes opened again. He stood completely still, and for a moment, it seemed not even the wildest of storms could ever move him again. For a second, the robot's eyes seemed to look at something entirely out of sight, almost as if he remembered the past before he zoomed back into reality and focused on his Commanding Officer. An idle smile covered his face.

"Manufacturer check finished. All outer functions are intact. My systems inform me, however, that I'm yet missing a personality and context chip as well as advanced coding instructions. Please upload the necessary information onto my software for me to be fully functional. I'm awaiting your orders, COCC."

"You really are just like the real thing, aye."

The Councillor grinned amusedly at the confused Robot 941120 and turned to the service robot who quietly stood in the corner, following the proceedings without a flicker of emotion on his face.

“Service, please upload the Council’s encrypted files onto Robot 941120’s system.”

“Of course, Councillor Christine.”

Christine turned towards her two bodyguards and gave them a knowing look. Almost gently, the two cows activated their mounted light MGs unbeknown to anyone but them. The targeting systems locked onto the robots. Better safe than sorry. One never knew what could happen during the upload. Especially with this one. He was so special, even unique. The last of his kind.

“All information is uploaded, Councillor.”

Christine nodded regally to the service robot.

“Robot 941120. Can you hear me?”

The robot opened his eyes which were now a fiery green.

“I am your Commanding Officer Councillor Christine.”

“I remember who you are, COCC.”

“Excellent. Welcome back to life, Robot 941120. You have been deactivated for a long time now. We have implemented an update onto your systems which will bring you up to speed on Paradise’s contemporary environment. Has the upload been successful?”

“Yes, Madame. It seems a lot has changed since my last update. All hail Paradise.”

“It has indeed, Robot 941120. We’ve come a long

time since the Last War, the expeditions beyond Sig's Canal and the very first First Councillor Emilia, the Great. Regardless of what has happened since then, we still stand strong and unwavering in the face of the unknown."

"We're nature's audacity."

Christine nodded slowly, and a sad smile covered her face, even reached for her eyes. It had been a long time since she had heard those words for the very first time.

A mantra she had lived by ever since. She would do anything to protect the great Paradise, the ultimate manifestation of survival and cooperation. She had sworn that a long time ago and now more than ever, she intended to keep her promise.

"I take it the Great Nine still live side by side with humanity then?"

"They do, though the foxes have created their own nation ever since your last activation."

The robot rolled his eyes playfully.

"Let me guess. They called it the Nation of Foxes or something like that."

"That's surprisingly accurate. But it's Fox Nation."

"Be that as it may, I'm glad to see all creatures harmoniously living together. It can't have been easy after all expeditions beyond Sig's Canal have been cancelled."

"Former First Councillor Thommy has always been short

sighted, and I'm certain he'll be on the wrong side of history. But for now, we haven't been beyond the Canal since the last expedition failed a long time ago. And today, we have a much bigger problem on our hands"

"I understand that from my updates, Madame."

The robot stretched and winked towards the bodyguarding cows behind the Councillor.

"No need to point those guns at me, Ladies. I couldn't harm you even if I wanted to."

The bodyguard cows stiffened.

"It's okay, girls. He's no danger."

A thin smile appeared on the robot's lips.

"Well then. Let's get to it. What's your name, Robot 941120?"

"My name is Helmut, COCC."

Christine nodded. It did seem like a randomly created name, though it had an odd German touch. Not what she had expected. It was a welcome surprise during a time where nothing much could surprise her anymore. It was time for the first real test.

"Welcome to the world, Helmut. Are you ready for your first order?"

"I am, Madame."

Helmut stood in front of her, his green eyes focused on her, just waiting for her next command. His body entirely naked, Christine caught herself staring at the muscles underneath his hybrid skin, the well-toned abs and the elegant hands which waited to execute her every command. He was reborn to serve, to serve her and nobody else. Adrenaline pumped through her veins and she felt euphoria rising in her four stomachs. Realisation poured onto her face when she recognised the feeling. She had always dismissed the idea before, but now that she was in charge of his creation, she finally understood after all this time.

"Do all of Paradise a favour, Helmut. Execute the service robot immediately. One public murder in 200 years is not enough for my taste."

If anyone else had been in the hangar, the Councillor's cold voice would have sent shivers down their backs. Robots, after all, were considered equal to humans and all other living creatures in Paradise.

Before the service robot could even make a disapproving sound, Helmut had turned around to him. With a sweeping motion, his hands found the service robot's head. A brutal jolt later, Helmut held the other robot's head in his hands. The eyes in this head, emptier than usual, stared right back at him. He carelessly dropped the head to the floor. Dust swirled up when the headless robot followed suit.

"Excellent. Only a dead robot is a good robot."

"Thank you, Madame."

"I assume you blocked his signals the moment you were brought to life?"

“Of course, Madame. Just as the code commanded me.”

The Councillor kicked the separated head like a football. With a clanking noise, it bounced off the wall.

“I always wanted to do that. Stupid robots.”

Helmut tilted his head and smiled ironically.

“Well, thank you, Madame. I take that as a compliment.”

“Not you, Helmut. You’re special. You’re nothing like him. You’re mine.”

“I live to serve, COCC.”

“I see the code also made you British,” Christine amusedly observed Helmut’s accent.

“I have a wide variety of accents at my disposal, Madame. But I prefer the British one. I consider it to be a funny addition to my name. I hope it will confuse people. A German speaking with an English accent.”

“I like it, Helmut. Keep up the good work.”

“Of course, Madame. What are your orders?”

“You are to find the killer of the murdered bull. You are to bring the killer to me. You are not to tell anyone except me about it. All other details can be found on your hard drive. The folder is called ‘The Fallen One’.”

“I am indeed in possession of such a folder, Madame. I will get to work right away.”

“Good luck, Helmut. Make me proud.”

“While I’m aware of what such a feeling is, I am

unable to experience it myself, Madame. Nonetheless, I will make you proud."

"Oh, and one last thing, Helmut. You'll meet your partner at the crime scene. Don't be fooled by her smile and positive mindset. She's a spy for the current First Councillor, who, frankly, is a pain in my arse. Make sure that she won't be a problem to me, you, or the investigation. Or anyone else."

"Of course, Madame. I'll handle her."

Councillor Christine nodded and watched the naked human-like robot leave the hangar. A single tear ran down her cheek.

Chapter Three

The Introduction

"You're him, aren't you?"

Helmut turned around to the bright voice behind him. He spotted the red-haired stranger approaching him.

Glock 19 on hip, left side. Extra sidearm, right calf. Two knives. Left ankle, hip. Hidden by dark leather jacket. Experienced in hand to hand combat. No known next of kin.

His systems continued to analyse the stranger while he answered.

"It is indeed I, Helmut", the former Robot 941120 proclaimed amusedly.

"It's an honour to meet you, Mr Helmut."

"The honour is mine. And who might you be?"

Helmut smiled knowingly. The Councillor had prepared him for such an occasion. His internal database had quickly found all relevant information on the stranger, but of course, he was designed to hide his crafty capabilities from the general public and his colleagues alike.

"I'm Susan, your partner in crime."

She looked at him.

Wrinkles around nose, left eyebrow lifted, lips slightly

opened, pupils wider than usual. Expectantly waiting.

Helmut's system analysed all of that in less than a second.

He laughed.

"Partner in crime. That's funny, Susan. That's really funny."

It wasn't.

Susan laughed.

"Well then. I was assigned to you by the Council. You're new here, aren't you?"

"Essentially just born", Helmut responded.

Susan laughed again. Humans had a tendency to ignore the obvious and call it sarcasm.

"You do look awfully young for your age."

"I'll take that as a compliment, Susan."

"As you should. They told me you were last stationed with our Embassy in North America?"

Cover story activated. Proceed with evasive step A.

"Indeed. But I'm not at liberty to talk about it, I'm afraid. Rest assured, the Clone Wars as we like to call them over there won't stop anytime soon. The Don's 69th clone has just been activated."

Susan ran her hand through the red hair on her head and looked around.

"Now then. What do we have here?"

The two stood in a well-lit tent which had been placed over the scattered remains of the former bull. The crime scene itself. Although the bull had fallen tens of storeys, the logistical unit of the local Police Department had managed to rebuild a 3D-projection of the bull just before the fall. Helmut took a step towards the lively projection, which unassumingly circled around the tent, unknowing of its demise. He looked almost alive.

"Why did you die, bull? Why did you die?"

The how was rather obvious, and the thought of that painted a fascinated smile on Helmut's face. Death was no stranger.

The bull silently stared back at him, the eyes empty and soulless.

"What are you doing?"

Susan appeared right behind the projection and carelessly walked through it. For a second, the bull was reflected on her human body, mixing them into a hybrid creature of sorts. It reminded Helmut of one of the old Greek myths.

The Centaur.

But as soon as the picture had emerged, it disappeared again and with it, all thoughts of it.

"You know the projection can't talk, right? Jesus Christ, what do they teach you in the south? That's where you're from, isn't it?"

"Relax, Susan. I'm just thinking out loud. Any theories?"

"Plenty, but none which fit the crime scene."

"What good are those then?"

"They entertain me while I watch you work, Helmut."

Helmut stepped outside the tent, expecting sunshine to greet him. Instead, cold northern winds had arrived early to the City. His hybrid skin showed goosebumps, though he didn't feel the cold. He tightened his scarf nonetheless. It was all about appearances.

"There is one theory I have, though."

"I'm all yours, Susan."

"The forensics report claims that the bull has been shot in the flanks and rear left leg before he fell out of the window. What if he didn't fall? What if he jumped?"

"And why would he do that? I read the report. He was gonna die either way. Those bullets were as precise as they can get."

"I don't know yet. Maybe he wanted to send some sort of message?"

Her voice sounded as uncertain as her posture indicated. After all this time, humans still hadn't learned to stop broadcasting their emotional state to anyone who watched close enough.

"Sounds… interesting."

Helmut nodded towards the bodyguard cows who had been assigned to him. For his protection, he was told by Christine. He laughed. For his protection. Rather to surveil him. Like he needed supervision.

"What's the deal with the cow unit anyway?"

"The Council granted the cows special access to our investigation because, well, the victim is a bull."

Susan didn't seem to spot the apparent lie behind Helmut's words.

"That seems logical enough. They could just have had a cow handle this if you ask me. There's no need to entertain our great minds."

"Let's check the other crime scene", Helmut deflected.

"Do we have to? We could just call it a day, you know?"

Hiding behind a massive wall of grey clouds, the sun swiftly set. Helmut wouldn't have noticed the slight difference in the darker shade of light without his robotic senses. It had been dark and grey even before the sun had set in the south. He stood tall by the broken window, just where a vast pool of blood had been only a few hours ago. He could almost feel the pain and suffering which the fallen bull must have experienced right here. He brushed his hair carelessly aside. He was so deeply absorbed by his thoughts that he almost didn't hear Susan stepping next to him.

"There's nothing really here, is there?"

"Nothing that hasn't already been included in the preliminary report."

Susan nodded her head.

Approvingly.

"Your turn. Any theories?"

"These carvings… I have seen them before."

A quick succession of pictures appeared in front of his inner eye. Too fast to analyse them. Too quick even for his senses. He'd need time. Time and a quiet space and all his resources.

Return to hangar for detailed analysis.

"Really? Where? Nobody knows what they mean. My tech guy said it took them ages to reconstruct them."

"I don't know," Helmut said much to his own surprise.

His systems ran on the highest speed and yet, he didn't know where he knew them from. Or even what they were.

Mysterious. Further investigation required.

"I just… I know I've seen them before. There's something about them. Something else entirely."

"You're speaking in riddles."

"It's probably nothing. Let me sleep on it. I might just be seeing ghosts."

"But then, if the killer had carved those markings into the bull's hide. Why? To torture him?"

"Why go through all that trouble? There are easier ways to make someone experience pain. Much easier, and much more pain."

"You have some sort of experience with that?"

"I read," Helmut laughed at her.

A quick succession of violent images appeared behind

his eyes. Violent and bloody.

Bleeding bodies, missing limbs, kneeling creatures, guns to their heads.

He shook his head, and the pictures were gone. Probably just a glitch in his systems. He'd have that checked out with the Councillor's medics later.

"So then, if not for torture. Why then mark those carvings into that poor bull?"

"Pity is misguided here."

"So, no ideas either then?"

Susan turned around to him, her eyebrow now lifted provocatively.

Challenging authority. Testing boundaries. Respond on a professional level.

"The only logical explanation would be that the killer wanted to send some sort of message through the carvings."

"That would explain why the bull jumped."

"Which, in turn, would mean that the killed bull knew what those markings meant."

"So, in conclusion, we have no idea what the fuck happened here?"

"Sounds about right, Susan."

Helmut gave Susan a slight smile.

"Why are you smiling then?"

"This was the first smart conversation we had."

Progress.

Susan rolled her eyes.

"No wonder they transferred you to the City with that sorta attitude."

Before Helmut could react, his phone rang.

"Would you excuse me for a second? I have to talk to my COCC."

"Your cock? What the fuck, Helmut? They didn't tell me you're the molesting type."

"Relax. My Commanding Officer Councillor Christine."

"Why didn't you say so?"

"I did, didn't I?"

His phone had stopped ringing by now, and it began to rain. Coincidence? Helmut was almost a hundred per cent certain of that.

"You said cock!"

"Jesus Christ, where did you grow up? The fifth republic?"

"I wish I was from that region. I was born and raised in what used to be Denmark."

Helmut laughed out loud.

"What? Did I say something funny?"

"Nah, it's nothing. It's just… my dear friend, we called him Syphilis for obvious reasons, used to stipulate that Denmark had no reason to exist. I'm finally beginning to see his point."

"Used to? What happened?"

Susan breezed right by Helmut's insult. He hadn't made any attempt to hide it. Susan was disturbingly immune to his efforts to get rid of her quickly.

"He died," he replied drily.

"Oh god, I'm sorry to hear that. Are you alright?"

"Yeah, don't worry. It was a long time ago."

"How did he die? If you don't mind me asking. But these sorta things made me become an investigator in the first place. It's just that there haven't been any murders, or dead people really, during my time in Paradise."

Helmut grinned. Finally, something he could identify with.

"A fire. He died in a fire, I've been told. Must have been gruesome really."

"I have never heard of any deadly fire for decades."

"Like I said, it's been a long time since then."

He recognised Susan's eyes on him.

Searching. Sceptical. Respond humorously.

Helmut gave her a wide smile.

"I'm just messing with you, Susan."

"Are you serious?"

"Of course. There hasn't been a deadly fire in decades. How could my dear friend Syphilis possibly have died there then?"

Susan rolled her eyes.

"And here I thought all humour was lost on you, Helmut."

"You'd be surprised how deep my understanding of the human mind reaches."

"I should have known by your friend's name. Syphilis. That's long extinct. Just like your not-so-dead friend, I reckon."

"My not-so-existing friend. I'm afraid he's nothing more than the product of my imagination."

With those words, he turned around and pretended to call Councillor Christine to update her.

Chapter Four

The Council

Scouting eagles flew high above the ground, overlooking the first funeral march Paradise had encountered since its creation. Thousands and thousands of cows walked through the streets, followed by robots, humans, apes and horses, dogs and cats. Even the donkeys had shown up, though they weren't quite sure why that was. Only a few foxes had joined them for they lived in isolation, far away from the City's shenanigans and nobody quite knew where the legendary Fox Nation was located. Their embassy was closed and had not yet issued a comment on yesterday's horrific incident which, of course, was the way the foxes usually reacted to anything ambiguous ever since they were granted vast autonomous rights to host their own nation within Paradise. The procession almost seemed to mock yesterday's happy celebrations by walking entirely in silence. Each of the participants carried a blue, glowing candle with them, showing their support to the fallen bull. They all walked towards the City's centre, where the bull had fallen from the building just yesterday.

Helmut had returned to his temporary home through the

tide of creatures making their way to the funeral march. The hangar where his COCC had awoken him didn't seem to have missed him. It was empty and quiet here, no living soul accompanied him. The dead robot's head still lay right where Councillor Christine had kicked it, and its body a mere few meters away. It was a small one at that, it would barely have reached Helmut's chest. He sensed the howling wind terrorising the City but it found no way through the thick walls and sealed doors. No light could reach into the vast halls, no windows offered a glimpse into the outside world. Helmut stood in the middle of the hangar, uncertain what to do. He felt tired, and though he knew he didn't need to sleep, he felt like it. There was something comforting about it which made him smile whenever he woke up. But there was no bed in the hangar yet, nor was there any sort of furniture. Helmut shrugged his shoulders and walked towards the holding cell where he placed his body in the retaining ring and closed his eyes. Then, he opened the 'Fallen Bull' folder as the Councillor had ordered him to and scrolled through its contents. One caught his attention.

Council Meeting on the Reactivation of Robot 941120.

Open.

Play.

Creatures of all of the Great Nine sat around a table in the middle of a vast room. Expansive glass windows allowed sunbeams to enter, flooding the room with bright light, almost too bright for the eye.

"I hereby declare the start of the monthly Council meeting", declared the First Councillor.

The members of the Council nodded approvingly. They all had been selected randomly by an algorithm, theoretically ensuring a perfectly proportional representation of Paradise's population. Long gone were the days of electoral democracy in favour of a truly democratic model.

"Foreign Affairs Councillor Ricky, please provide your report for today's Session before the Senate."

"Honoured Councillors, I will keep this brief so that we can all move on to the most pressing issue of the day. Following yesterday's 200th anniversary of the Creation of Paradise, our home is flourishing. We remain self-sufficient on all frontiers, the happiness scale developed by our friends in the Science Department shows that our citizens are entirely happy with the current state of Paradise and our carbon footprint remains positive. All in all, Paradise remains in a strong and safe position. Our borders remain secure, and the population is not concerned with what is happening across the Atlantic. We find ourselves entangled in continuing negotiations with the League, but we should see progress on this front in the upcoming months. Our diplomats are confident to secure an agreement with the Free Cities soon. To our

East, Sig's Canal remains heavily fortified, and our robot units report no activity on the other side, neither do our scouting eagles. It would appear that after all this time, there are no living creatures to the East anymore, which could threaten Paradise and penetrate our borders. All hail Paradise. Our units will, of course, remain stationed there and we have additionally sent a cow regiment to the Canal to patrol alongside the stationed robots. It is tranquil for this time of the year. They're accompanied by scouting eagles to provide aerial surveillance. The neighbourhood to the South remains a nuclear wasteland. We have not registered activity there for over 100 years. However, we would recommend adding extra sea mines across the shores to ensure no unwanted surprises arise. Always remember that we didn't see the Last War coming, and it almost brought us to our knees. Across the Atlantic, the civil war continues to rage throughout Northern America with no end in sight. Our Agency spies report that the 69th clone of the Don continues to hold the East coast, while California continues to fight for independence. We should not be too concerned with the former superpower recovering from the devastating blow that was WWIII for them. However, be that as it may, we would suggest sending our Foreign Legion to California's aid. Keeping an equilibrium in the Second American Civil War will aid us in our safety. A reunited North America could potentially threaten our grip on essential resources which we currently enjoy on the African continent. Our colonies remain unrivalled and with no surviving life forms found yet, we shall continue to harvest everything we need."

"Thank you, Councillor Ricky. The Council will consider your recommendation and decide on next week's Council meeting."

"Thank you, First Councillor."

"Anything noteworthy in the bi-annual report on Paradise? It appears to be quite extensive."

"Yes, First Councillor", the Eagle responded.

"Our archaeologists believe that they have found the remains of the Kaiserpaar, though more tests are needed to come to feasible conclusions. Moreover, we have picked up chatter about a zealous religious underground group and references to pre-Paradise legends. We have introduced Agency agents into their organisation and we're eager to learn more about them. It's been quite a while since we last heard about anything of that kind. I'm also glad to announce that the Independent State of California has accepted our preliminary Eagle regiment aid and has incorporated them into their army. They will shortly provide us with more reliable information than our current sources on the ground ever could."

"Thank you, Councillor Erian. That concludes the official part of this meeting. Which only leaves what we all came here to discuss. Yesterday's incident. How does the Council suggest to handle it? I've been told by Secretary Justine that the relevant Council members have been meeting on this issue beforehand."

"First Councillor, the Council appreciates your concern on this matter and has concluded that this incident requires a thorough investigation with no public oversight. We, therefore, suggest a different approach rather than activating our newest police robots for this", the Robot Councillor Felicitas reported.

"Councillor Felicitas, what would this solution entail then? I don't see any solution other than using our police robots for this. Maybe we can accompany them with a multi-creature task force?"

"First Councillor, the respective Councillors suggest reactivating Robot 941120 for this matter."

"Robot 941120, are you serious?"

For the first time in today's session and possibly ever, the First Councillor's voice lost its composure. His face turned pale and ugly. A matter that was not aided by his lack of any facial hair.

"Yes, Sir."

"Remind me again, but wasn't that particular robot discontinued after it had rejected a shooting order at Sig's Canal?"

"Yes, Sir. Since then, a new software update has been installed, and no other incidents occurred. Yet, former

First Councillor Thommy discontinued Robot 941120 after the incident out of fear of it recurring. This model, however, is our most advanced model yet. We haven't researched anything like it since then, on orders of former First Councillor Thommy whose fear significantly set back our AI advancements. There is nothing to rival it. Hence, we strongly believe that Robot 941120 is needed for this. Besides, nobody outside this Council knows about its existence."

"And all Councillors share this belief?"

"Aye."

"What is the reasoning for this proposal?"

There was no hesitation in her voice.

"First Councillor. This incident is the first time since the Creation of Paradise that there has been any bloodshed on our soil. The very first time. So far, the public believes this was an accident, or according to one conspiracy theory, a suicide. We have limited any access to the body, and only very few know that it was neither. We have a murder on our hands, First Councillor, and we know nothing about it. We can't use the usual channels to investigate this, and none of our resources are equipped to do this quietly anyhow. This entire institution has been built on transparency but the public isn't ready for the truth yet. It would create chaos in Paradise. We need something unknown which won't cause concern. Robot 941120 is unknown to the public.

There are no public records of its existence. He will be recoded for our purposes and answer directly to us. Nobody will ever learn what we don't want them to know. And while we would not usually approve of such action, we believe that it is necessary. For the safety of Paradise, and for the good of our citizens."

The First Councillor sighed.

"Then it is hereby decided. We shall reactivate Robot 941120 to investigate the circumstances of 'the accident of the Fallen Bull' as the public has come to know the incident. Act with utmost caution."

"Of course, First Councillor. Thank you."

"Who will oversee Robot 941120?"

"Given the circumstances, I would suggest that Cow Councillor Christine oversees this investigation."

"All those who agree that Councillor Christine should take charge of this investigation, please say aye."

"Aye", the Council responded without any objections.

Councillor Christine nodded thankfully and gently walked towards the hall's gate. Her long, dark robe followed her like the dark shadow, which slowly approached on Paradise's horizon. A lazy smile appeared on Christine's lips. There was work to be done in the shadows, where she felt most comfortable.

Chapter Five

The Headquarters

"Here you go."

Susan cheerfully smiled towards Helmut and handed him a portable cup.

"What's that?"

"What's that, he says. It's coffee."

Helmut hesitated slightly almost as if he couldn't quite follow what was happening.

"Well, thanks, I guess."

Sceptical. Analysing creature and content.

"There we go. Was that so hard?"

"I didn't ask for the coffee, did I?"

"No, but you got one nonetheless."

"It's a bit like paying taxes and then receiving new lights instead of the sidewalk you were hoping for."

"You didn't even give me any money, Helmut. It's a surprise."

Expectant eyes. Slightly straighter shoulders. Attentive.

"I'm no fan of surprises."

"I'm not surprised."

"Guess, none of us is surprised then."

Susan continued to smile, utterly disregarding his

moody reaction as she always did.

"Come now, Helmut. At least try it."

Helmut rolled his eyes, smiled sourly and took a sip from the cup.

Unknown liquid. Assessing. Not dangerous. Proceed.

"It's not bad."

Susan drank some of her cup and turned to Helmut.

"Not bad, he says. The gods sent their angels to introduce us to coffee. It's the only good thing that ever happened to us."

"Except, of course, surviving the Last War, living in Paradise, and investigating the first and only murder in said Paradise."

"Except that, of course", she nodded.

"I could go on. That list is unending."

"Whatever, Helmut. Besides, it's much better coffee than the one they serve over there."

Susan pointed to the expansive building in front of them. Despite the glass front, Helmut's sharp eyes couldn't identify what was happening on the inside. It stood vast and tall almost as if it was reaching for the grey and cloudy sky above it.

Deflecting materials detected.

"I've never been. First day in the office."

"Don't worry, Helmut. I got your back."

Through the doors into the wide entrance hall, passing by the security gate, into the elevator, up to the 13th floor, into the office. Helmut's systems ran hot while processing all the new information. Eagles circling the building, huge cows in front of the entrance, mounted with heavy MGs, a few police robots standing guard by the security gate, regular humans by the elevators. Drunk donkeys in the holding cells. Slightly ashamed stallions coming to pick them up. Mares inquiring about the latest developments, cats and dogs freely roaming through the welcoming area, looking for nothing in particular. He even recognised the shape of an ape on the floor, taking a relaxing nap. His snores resounded from the high ceiling. Then, the door to his office shut, and with that, all the sounds and impressions disappeared.

"Welcome to your office, Helmut."

A dog stood upright on his rear legs, his tail waving through the air.

"How did you get up so quickly? I hadn't even passed the door yet when you welcomed me."

The dog smiled and barked excitedly.

"Excuse the barking, Sir. I smelled your arrival."

"You smelled me?"

"Yes, Sir. You and Susan, in fact. My kind has learnt to speak and walk upright, but we haven't lost our original gifts."

"So, if I threw a bone out of the window, you'd jump after it?"

The dog's smile froze and he came back down to all

fours without making a sound.

"Sir?"

"I'm just messing with you. Thanks for this wonderful welcome."

The dog's tail began to move again and he jumped into his chair behind the desk, placing his paws on the keyboard in front of him. He almost disappeared behind the wide screen on his desk..

"Thanks, Caspar."

"Of course, Susan. Everything is prepared as we have discussed earlier."

"If you'd follow me, Helmut."

Susan entered yet another room and closed the door behind him. Helmut found himself standing in a tall space with high ceilings and big glass windows. Grey clouds greeted him from the outside.

"This is quite something, isn't it?"

He turned to the ever-excited and smiling Susan, who stood a few steps away.

"Did you decorate this?"

"I did indeed."

Helmut nodded while his eyes quickly jumped to the objects in the room. A painting on the wall caught his attention.

"What's that?"

"Ah, I somehow suspected this one would interest you. It's a painting from the last expedition across the

Canal in the beginnings of Paradise."

"Back when we still dared to explore the unknown."

"Back when we were just recovering from the Last War and had to fight for our immediate survival."

"Who painted it?"

"Nobody quite knows," Susan whispered cryptically.

"So, you know but won't tell me."

Susan laughed delightedly.

"Nobody actually quite knows. I'm serious for once. It just appeared in the national museum one day. Caused a huge stir back then, because the mission was technically classified."

"It's just a painting though, isn't it?"

"Of course, but it's depicting the last ever expedition across the Canal."

"The expedition wasn't public?"

"No, and neither were its outcomes at the time."

"But it's been confirmed to depict real events?"

"Yes. The Council reluctantly informed the public about the expedition afterwards when the painting appeared. It's been rumoured that Tim Corps himself created it."

"Tim Corps? The founder and CEO of Timcorps Enterprises? He's been dead since forever."

"He committed suicide shortly afterwards when TCE went bankrupt."

"I hate when people throw away their lives like that."

"Indeed. He was the most brilliant mind Paradise ever entertained. This is supposedly his final design."

Helmut stepped closer to the wall and studied the painting intensely.

He recognised the bird's-eye perspective from which it must have been painted. A vast body of water ran in the background, a wild mix of blue and white.

On the other side of the Canal, on Paradise's side, stood a massive fortress. It almost seemed to have been built in the Dark Ages, only the newer materials gave it away. Solar panels covered the few roofs inside the fortress, instead of archers, sound cannons were mounted to the walls and a massive radar-station stood tall in the middle of it all. The old Alliance flag hung in the wind. Snow-covered mountains complemented the background, providing an almost impenetrable path to Paradise. He recognised the few creatures standing guard on the tall walls, carrying rifles and field glasses, wearing the blue colours of the Alliance. The sun rose hot in the sky, raining down sunbeams like bombs. A vast and thick green forest stretched across the rest of the painting, painstakingly detailed trees emerged in Helmut's sight, each more various than the last, their leaves dense and then light, sometimes green, then a bit darker than that, until it almost appeared as if all light disappeared in the forest, as if the woods absorbed all brightness and left nothing but despair and darkness behind. At the entrance of the forest, coming off a transport boat, a squad of soldiers moved towards the forest. Instead of the blue colours of the fortress guards, they wore dark shades which seemed to change colour depending on where they stood. Some were just leaving the ship, their weapons tucked to their backs, while others were midways to the forest and a few were already standing between the trees, carefully observing their surroundings. They wore uniforms of no particular colour, seemingly fading into the background. Then, suddenly, out of nowhere, the painting moved, and a huge monster appeared next to the soldiers, apparently ready to attack them any second.

Helmut was startled and quickly jumped away from the picture.

For a moment, the creature looked like a lion, but when Helmut focused his entire attention on the beast, it turned out to be a mere tall and fluffy dog.

He took a deep breath and reanalysed the painting. The dog didn't move, nor did it seem to startle the soldiers at all. After a few long seconds, he realised that he just overlooked the fluffy dog at first. It looked so innocent and cute between the grim soldiers, between the weapons and thick forest, between Paradise and the unknown. Innocent and cute and utterly misplaced.

"What's it called?", he asked into the silence.

“Look to the far left”, Susan gently whispered.
Helmut turned his head slightly.
Here be dragons.

Chapter Six

Snowy Confusion

It was early in the morning when Helmut walked towards the Councillor's offices. A few days had passed since his activation, and so far, he had found no way to solve the murder just yet. He had spent the past nights back in the hangar, which, according to Councillor Christine, was only temporary until her office had found him a suitable apartment in the centre of the City. He didn't mind staying in the hangar. It wasn't in his nature to be attached to anything. His code wasn't written for that sort of purpose, and neither was he.

The snow squeaked shrill under his boots. Since it started snowing half a day ago, it hadn't stopped. The snowflakes stood out brightly against the dark sky above him. Helmut could identify every falling flake above him, he could count them, sort them, categorise them. But to what end? It would have only taken up needless storage in his memory drive which was anchored deeply in the centre of his chest. There wasn't anyone on the streets this early, especially with this sort of weather catching the City entirely by surprise and so Helmut let his thoughts wander a little. Away from his ever-so-squeaking steps towards last night's dream. Ever since

Councillor Christine had brought him to life he had experienced odd dreams. There was something about them he couldn't quite catch. Something real, something tangible, something different all together. They were bloody, they were dark, and they were oddly familiar. And then, there were the carvings, the way of the execution, and the jump out of the window. Helmut knew he had too little information to draw any conclusions just yet, or ever, if his investigations continued at the current speed, but the carvings also seemed familiar. But to what end had they been carved into the bull? And for what purpose had the bull jumped? All he knew so far was that he knew nothing of importance. All he had to show for his investigation so far were a few dreams and wild speculations. Somehow the murder, the carvings and the jump were all connected, but how? He almost felt like he had seen the carvings before, almost felt like he had seen the exact same scene once before. But, of course, that was impossible. There must be an explanation, a natural connection that currently escaped him.

Disappointing.

As he walked, Helmut left a trail of footprints behind him which was covered by newly fallen snow almost immediately. Despite the cold temperatures and the wet snow, Helmut didn't feel a thing. His outer body showed all the necessary symptoms of being on the outside but inside, a well-oiled machinery continued to pump hot energy rays through his electronics. Snow covered the usually colourful houses around the City's main square, surrounding the lonely Helmut with nothing but wet grey, leaving an empty, hollow, aimless shell behind. There was nothing here for him that would help him solve the crime he was quite literally born to solve. Helmut felt a heavy figurative blanket around his shoulders which seemed to drag him towards the cold ground rather than warm him. Why did the execution seem so familiar? He didn't know that yet, but what he did know was that it must have been an execution. He didn't know why, but he knew that. Helmut sank to the ground absentmindedly and before he knew it, the snow began to cover him.

"Why's your hair so wet? And your clothes? Your trousers? Are you alright, Helmut?"

Helmut gently smiled at Councillor Christine's secretary. The cow had managed to somehow sit behind a desk which had apparently explicitly been designed for anything but cows.

Equality my arse.

"Of course, Volker. I'm alright. I just fell on my way here. Must have been the only uncovered ice floe in the entire City that I somehow managed to step on."

"You must be freezing. Let me get you some fresh

clothes and a blanket or two."

Helmut hesitated for a moment.

"Yes, I guess I must be freezing. Please be so kind as to fetch me those things."

"Right away, Helmut."

The door to Councillor Christine's office opened before Volker came back and Helmut stepped into her office, dripping wet snow. *The Wet Robot* would probably have been an excellent title for a porn movie these days.

"Well, you certainly look like you had a great time outside. What did ya do?"

"Ah, you know. The usual. Just fought a few foxes and humped a donkey, COCC."

Councillor Christine nodded somewhat amused and yet fascinated by Helmut's appearance.

"Enough with the chitchat. What can you tell me about the incident?"

"It's definitely a murder."

Councillor Christine looked at Helmut.

Expectantly. Not amused. Empty face.

The amusement had left her face as quickly as the rats had left Tschernobyl.

"You've had five days since your activation, and that's everything you came up with? 'It's definitely a murder'. Are you fucking kidding me?"

"Councillor, with all due respect, there's not a lot to

go on. We have a body splintered across the four corners of Paradise, a hollow projection of what used to be the victim, and odd carvings in his hide."

"That's all? Is there no ballistics report? No DNA traces? No nothing?"

High pitched voice. On edge. Respond cautiously. Fact-based.

"No, Councillor. The ballistics report states that there isn't a bullet in the body which, essentially, should be impossible. We haven't found any DNA traces which either means it was a robot, a creature in a bodysuit or a sniper, and we absolutely have no clue as to why the bull fell through the window. Of course, it can't be a sniper because that would neglect the carvings. So it's reasonable to assume that it was either a robot or a creature in a bodysuit. Unless, of course, the victim carved those markings onto his hide himself. All of which doesn't help us much. We're checking CCTV footage consistently, but there's just too much traffic to identify a potential perpetrator just yet."

"What about the victim?"

"His name is Luciano Franculo, going by the nickname 'the Italian sausage'. Apparently he had a reputation for a wild party life and all the things that come with it. He was also very passionate about Sig's Canal and Paradise's isolation, though he appears to have been the only one in the entire world concerned with that. On this side of the border, anyway. Other than that, all data suggests he lived an ordinary life. Susan talked to his next of kin, and she hasn't found anything suspicious. We'll be attending his funeral to see whether there's anything we missed. The body is currently prepared to be returned to his family. We've created a second report which states he was drunk when he fell out of the window. It was a festive day after all. I'm sure the family will be devastated."

"What about the carvings?"

Helmut faltered for a second, the second time today.

Most unusual behaviour. Run check.

"Nothing. Nobody knows what they are or why they were carved onto the victim."

"Jesus Christ. So, are there any working theories then?"

Calm voice. Fact-based answer successful. Noted. Proceed.

"Yes. One. But with very little to go on. We believe that the victim jumped out of the window on his own account. Why, we don't know yet, but we assume that it is linked to the markings carved onto his hide. We can't be certain what they mean, but we have theorised that they're the reason why the bull jumped out of the window. Our current idea is that the carvings are some sort of message or secret code."

"By that logic, then the victim must have known what

they were, or at least understand their significance."

"Indeed. Which creates more questions than answers really. But it's something to start with. I'm currently analysing the carvings but so far haven't found anything substantial."

"Okay. Continue in that direction. And get rid of Susan. She's a stupid surveillance by the First Councillor, and I can't have anyone interfering here, am I clear?"

"Of course, Madame."

"Good. Is there anything else then?"

Helmut took a deep breath.

"Yes, one thing. You said I was supposed to come to you if I experienced anything odd…"

"Well?"

Before Helmut could raise his voice again, the Councillor's phone rang.

"Excuse me, Helmut. I have to get this. It's the First Councillor."

"Of course, Madame."

"We'll get on this right away again."

"Don't worry, Madame. It's not urgent. It's nothing really."

"Alright. I'll see you later then."

Chapter Seven

The Questioning

Helmut chucked his coffee, then tossed his cup carelessly aside. It had been a frustrating day so far, even for a robot.

"Anything?"

He shook his head and turned around to Susan.

"I got nothing off them."

"Me neither."

"It's like they're all telling the same story, reading from the same script."

"Do you think that's a coincidence?"

"Pretty much, yeah. He seems to have been just a regular citizen. There's nothing to suggest anything different so far. I haven't yet seen a single shred of evidence why he might have been targeted. Absolutely nothing. I wish there were something."

"Don't get me wrong. I love that we live in such peaceful and happy times, but at least back then, there was just more action… and more leads. And a bit more action, I've been told."

The latter made Helmut smile.

"You were present then, aye. Back in the Wild West when gunslingers ruled and reigned."

"Oh yeah, most definitely. Good times. I was the best at it, too. Everybody feared me and my gunslinging abilities."

A police robot interrupted their banter.

"We got a new group ready for you. Close friends and family this time. They look tired though."

"Thank you."

Helmut got up.

"The most promising bunch yet."

"And the last of them. Finally."

"And how do you know Luciano?"

"He was my cousin, Sir."

Sir.

Helmut smiled gently.

"Relax, kiddo. We just want to ask a few questions. Nothing more."

The kid in front of him didn't relax. Her eyes nervously ran around the empty room.

"This does look like an interrogation room."

"That's because it is. But don't worry. We're just a bit stretched today. The Police Department isn't used to so much work."

"I'm glad to hear that."

"Tell me, then. Was there anything suspicious about Luciano in the last few days."

The kid seemed to think for a few seconds. Her eyes

shifted a little.

Recalling events.

"No, nothing. Sir. In fact, I haven't even seen him over the past few days to be honest. He would just disappear without warning and only be back after a few days. Once he left for two weeks and did not tell a soul."

"Yeah, I noticed that."

"I'm sorry I can't be of more help, but everything seemed normal, until…"

Tears began to fill her eyes.

Helmut resisted the urge to roll his eyes and handed her a few tissues.

"Were you guys close?"

"More than most. He was a good soul. Gentle. I really enjoyed it whenever he was around."

That, too, was a recurring feature of the investigations. Nobody quite seemed to dislike him.

"Is there anything else you might remember?"

"Nothing, Sir."

"Okay. Thanks for coming in today. If there's anything you remember, feel free to call the Department. There's also a free psychologist available to you if you feel the need to talk about your feelings."

"Thank you, that's very kind, Sir."

The kid got up and walked towards the door, her daringly bright clothes a vast contrast to the otherwise grey room.

Helmut quickly added the conversation to the relevant folder where it was met with all of today's interrogations. They had been fruitless.

He's a gentle soul.

Kind.

Funny.

He was interested in the Canal.

Never hurt anybody.

He liked to party but was very respectful.

Girlfriend? No, he preferred ponies.

Sometimes he would go on about Sig's Canal.

The kid turned around and looked at Helmut.

"There's one thing, though."

Helmut's head went up immediately.

"What is it?", he asked as gently as possible not to spook her.

"It was a while back. It's nothing really. I don't think it's relevant. But sometimes, when he was drunk, he'd go on about his passion for the Canal and the Badlands beyond it."

"A few others mentioned it, but it never sounded serious."

"It wasn't really until a few weeks ago. He came home one day, his eyes glowing. He was going on and on about the Canal."

"Do you remember what it was about?"

"Not really. I was super sleepy and had a big test the

next day. But I remember he said he'd want to see the place where it all took part. Beyond the Canal. Do you think that's relevant? But then again, he's always had periods where he was super keen on anything before the Last War."

"It might be, but it seems nothing but a bit of day-dreaming, in my opinion."

"Probably. He never mentioned it before or after again anyway."

"Well then, it's probably nothing more. But in case you should remember more, please let us know."

Helmut handed her a card.

The little girl held it tightly with her tiny fingers. "Of course."

"Thank you. Bye now."

"That's it for the day, it seems. Anything interesting mentioned in your conversations?"

Susan slightly tilted her head.

"Nothing, really. Apparently, he seemed extra keen on stories about pre-WWIII stuff lately."

"Same, but I've been told that his passion came and went every now and then."

"Do we note it in the report regardless?"

"I don't think we have to. We'll just add the transcripts of the conversations and highlight where to find further information. Should be enough."

"It's a pity really. He seemed to be a really good guy. For a bull, that is."

Helmut grinned.

"Are you getting sentimental in your old age?"

"Are you calling me old?"

"No, absolutely not. You're clearly the other thing. The opposite. Wait, what's that?"

"Young and agile?"

"No, just super old. That's the opposite of old."

"Are you calling me ancient now?"

"I could imagine you've been called worse things in your life."

"Probably have been," she laughed him off.

Oddly immune to insults. Recalculating.

Together, they left the Police Department. Cold wind welcomed them outside. Helmut tightened his scarf which was coloured in Paradise's colours. His own little tribute to the almighty Creation.

"Another wasted day at the office then."

"Quite literally," Susan laughed.

"Any plans for tonight?"

"Nothing really. I just moved here so I might decorate my new place a little more. Hang up pictures, move furniture. That sorta thing. What about you?"

"Probably just gonna grab a bite to eat and then head home."

"Sounds delightful."

A thought occurred to Helmut.

Potentially lonely.

He scanned Susan from the side. She didn't seem to notice and brought her hood over her head.

"Do you want to go for a drink?"

Susan stared at him for a second, utterly shocked.

"Oh no, not like that. Just a drink between colleagues. I don't know about you, but it's been a long and frustrating day for me and I could really use one."

Her shoulders relaxed a bit, though her eyes were still narrow and inquiring.

Once an investigator, always an investigator.

"I guess one wouldn't hurt. Got a place in mind?"

"Nah, not really. Believe it or not, the thought just occurred to me."

Susan grinned.

"What about that one then?"

She pointed to a small alley. At the end of it lay the shadowy entrance to a bar.

The Highlands.

Chapter Eight

The Epiphany

"Given that we'll be stuck with each other for a while, I figured we might as well get to know each other a little better."

"On the current speed of our investigation, we'll probably spend years together in this bar."

Helmut and Susan raised their glasses. A bitter liquid ran down Helmut's throat.

"Bloody hell. I let you choose any drink of your choosing, and you chose tequila?"

"You're welcome," Susan giggled.

"So, what do you make of our case then?"

Susan shook her head.

Disapproving.

"You lured me into here with the promise to talk about anything but the case, remember? Quite frankly, I've had enough of this case for today. It's a bloody one-way street, and that's the last we'll talk about it today."

"My apologies. The case is the only thing getting me out of bed these days. What else would you like to talk about then?"

"Anything but your cock."

Gentle tone. Teasing. Proceed playfully.

"I've heard that before, I'm not gonna lie."

Susan couldn't help herself but laugh.

Measured self-deprecation successful. Noted.

A rock band softly played their first tunes of the night on the stage. The lights had already been dimmed, offering only light fades of red, turning the bar into a mystical place.

"This place reminds me of the Scottish highlands. It's dark, empty and the red light makes it look like a rogue battlefield. Just like the sunsets over there."

"Others would call this romantic, but it reminds you of a battlefield."

"That's exactly my sort of romantic."

"You must have served too long. How long were you with the Diplomatic Corps?"

Backstory activated. Proceed honestly with a hint of regret.

"From the beginning, really. My dad served on the protective detail of one of our Ambassadors. Mum was a lawyer on the mission. That's how they met, my parents. They always told me it was love at first sight. I grew up behind thick walls and around heavy artillery. It's not pretty out there, especially in the Colonies down south. But you get used to it. There's an entire world out there that we don't know about. A wracked world nonetheless. Over time, it all just becomes a game. Until the game ends, and real life sets in. When it got too real, we moved back to Paradise. But once I was back, this place, for all its perfection, it bored me. I was bored day in, day out and nobody understood why. After all, we had it all, didn't we? We lived in Paradise. But it wasn't my Paradise. It wasn't what I wanted for my life. So, when I was old enough, I signed up and did my military service before I moved to the Diplomatic Corps."

"Quite impressive. I know of very few people who actually still went to the military. I always thought that was rather a place for robots and bulls who are still trying to earn their credentials."

"It is, but it was the right place for me. And it gave me a deeper appreciation for both robots and bulls. Besides, flying on an eagle's back is worth the years eating nothing but mud at the Canal."

"You flew on an eagle's back?" Susan exclaimed loudly.

Helmut blushingly cautioned her, but it was too late. The bartender already looked over. Then, after a short moment of consideration, came over.

"That's my childhood dream," she inserted herself into the conversation.

Fascinated. Slightly hopeful. Honest. Proceed dominantly.

"It's a feeling you'll never forget. The wind on your face, the feathers in your hand, the sheer nothingness above the skies. Incredible! I think I still have the video at home. I'll bring it some time."

"That'd be great. I'd love to see it."

"And to whom would I be showing it?"

"You'd be showing it to Neshama, tonight's bartender at your service," the bartender playfully responded.

"Well, Neshama, it'd be my pleasure. Until then, could we get two more of those, please?"

Helmut pointed to the empty glasses in front of them.

"Sure. Be right back."

Susan exhaled loudly.

"Aren't you the smooth talker?"

"I have my moments," Helmut grinned devilishly.

"I can see that. Just don't try your luck on me. You'd burn your pretty face."

"Aw, you think I'm pretty? How generous, Susan."

"The most generous."

Repetitive use of wrong grammar. Plays with language. Comfortable.

"Indeed. Now it's your turn. Tell me something about you."

Susan took a deep breath.

Heavy story anticipated. Prepare to comfort.

"Here it is, my story. I grew up in a tiny town in the North, a few clicks from the ruins of Copenhagen. There was nothing there really. Probably the opposite of your childhood. The only entertainment I had were stories. The first one I was ever told was about the three iconic

Titans and their fight against the Greek gods. My grandma told me that one and many more. I can't stress enough how much I loved those stories.

Wrong assessment. Re-calculating.

"Later, I started to read and would read anything that I could find. It didn't matter what. Crime, Fiction, Sci-Fi, Fantasy. Whatever survived the war. Those were my favourites. The old ones. The old books. I rarely found any, and if I did, they were difficult to read, but one day, by sheer luck, my mum had sent me out to play with some kids. I got lost in the snowy forest and couldn't find my way back. Until suddenly, I fell into a deep well. It should have broken my neck, but instead, I found myself in an old bunker which survived the war but was forgotten afterwards. And there it was, a library. Must have been some rich people's bunker or something. Every story I could have ever imagined lay right in front of me. So I activated my SOS-tracker, started a bright, hot fire and began to read. When my parents found me, they could barely take me away from the library. I would go back more often than I could count. First to the dismay of my parents, later with their permission."

Re-calculation concluded. Insufficient data to proceed. Caution.

"Ultimately, those stories drove me to study criminology. A useless program in a place which hasn't seen an exciting crime since its Creation, but a degree nonetheless. I was assigned to the usual stuff, mostly missing persons which sounds very interesting until you realise that it's mostly old people who have lost their way."

Susan laughed a bright laugh.

"I'm glad I'm here now. Even under these circumstances. But enough about me. Let's get wasted."

"Cheers," Helmut agreed and lifted his glass.

Helmut watched Susan leave through the door.

Uncertainty. Reassessing data.

Before he could analyse tonight's collected data, the bar's lights dimmed even further until even his robotic eyes could barely see anything. Then, suddenly, as quick as lightning, a four-legged creature in sparkling clothes jumped onto the stage. The dim light brightly reflected the sparkles, blinding Helmut for a second. When he regained complete control over his eyesight again, he exhaled, astonished. The most beautiful creature he had ever seen in his life danced on the stage.

Admirable. Astonishing. Astounding. Simply majestic.

The audience cheered the dancing cow loudly. Helmut found himself standing without even realising it. Her movements were so agile, so quick, so precise. He shook himself. What was happening?

Analysing. Analysing. Analysing.

Helmut downed his drink and turned to Neshama.

"Who's that?"

"The stripping cow?"

"Yes, the dancing one!"

Neshama laughed gently.

"Don't worry. She calls herself the Stripping Cow. Her name is Marguerite."

Marguerite.

"That's a beautiful name," he whispered to himself while Neshama refilled his glass.

Up on the stage, Marguerite began to strip her sparkling clothes off, revealing her extra short hide she carried underneath.

She was greeted with loud cheers by the audience. Helmut bobbed his head to the sound of the music and watched how Marguerite moved to its rhythm.

Graceful. Grandiose. Grand.

"Yeah, she's quite something, this one."

Neshama set Helmut's glass next to him. It was filled with a bright blue liquid.

"You know her well?"

"Do I know her well? She's my roommate", Neshama laughed.

Helmut just nodded speechlessly.

Warning. System overload imminent.

"Tell you what. If you let me fly on one of your eagles, I might introduce you to her."

Warning. Warning. System overload imminent.

Helmut felt the hot energy rays pump through his body, felt how the cooling systems were quickly overpowered, felt water drip down his hybrid skin.

He downed his drink yet again to provide his systems with more liquid. It tasted oddly sweet.

"That sounds like a fair deal. But I have a better idea."

"Better than that? Impossible!"

"I'm gonna go dance with her."

Helmut turned around to Neshama.

Speechless.

"But I'm sure we'll manage the eagle thing, don't worry."

Liar.

Then, Helmut walked towards the stage.

Determination.

He felt his systems re-taking control, finally cooling his overheating body. Every step felt like an earthquake, shook Helmut to the core, shook his entire belief system to the core. Then, he jumped onto the stage.

Warning. Warning. Warning.

Chapter Nine

The Confusion

A burning ship on the sea. A blue sky at night. A calm ocean. Utter silence. A projection appears in front of my eyes. Full and strong, aesthetic and agile, real and imagined.

"Run, brother, run."

Flames appear in the projection, seem to reach for Syphilis.

"We have been betrayed. Run far, brother, farther than you have ever run."

"Syphilis, what is happening?"

My voice sounds weak and fragile. I'm confused. I don't understand what is happening.

"We've been betrayed."

The fire reaches for Syphilis who jumps out of its way. Sweat runs down his hybrid skin and desperation stands in his eyes.

"Why am I not with you? Where are you?"

"We've been separated. You're our only hope now. Run and hide. Cross the Canal."

"No, I can see you. I see the ship. I can save you."

I start running towards the burning vessel on the ocean. I can reach it, I can save Syphilis, I can save my brothers and sisters. I know it.

"No. You must run. It's too late for us. We've been betrayed by our masters."

I cut through the cold wind, feel wet drops on my face, feel the pain.

The faster I run, the further the burning ship appears to be. I can't reach it, yet I hear the screams. I can't reach it, yet I feel the pain. I can't reach it, yet I suffer the deaths.

"I'm coming for you. I'm gonna get you out of there."

An imploring smile appears on Syphilis' face.

"No, you won't. You're the last of us. We're long gone when you experience this."

I don't understand. I can't answer him. I'm running even faster now. The projection continues to be by my side.

The angle widens. I can see other robots trying to escape the large container, which is slowly melting. I can feel the heat on my skin just as they must feel it on theirs. It is unbearably hot. Even our hybrid skin can't take it anymore. I watch their desperate faces while they try to open the doors, attempt to extinguish the flames. But they're not successful. They can't be by nature. We weren't created for this purpose. I know all of that, and yet hope remains in my heart.

"Tumleh, listen to me carefully. When you're experiencing this, that means you've been activated. The

Council would only do that in particular circumstances. You're in danger. Paradise is in danger. A silent war wages through Paradise since its Creation. No matter what you hear about our purpose, don't trust it."

The flames have now reached Syphilis. He lifts his left arm and shows me a tattoo. He silently stands there, waiting for me to recognise the fine dark lines on his arm. My eyes focus on the intertwined lines. They seem so random, yet so familiar. Then I recognise them. My legs unwillingly stop working. I fall down, my hybrid skin tears open, blood flows out of the wound. The tattoo. The carvings on the murdered bull. They're the same. I get back to my feet, still in shock.

"Trust your instincts. Trust your feelings. Find the Centaur."

Syphilis' voice is soft and distant now, almost weak. His projection becomes thinner by the second until ultimately, I can see right through him onto the burning ship.

"Goodbye, brother. Remember me. Long may Paradise reign."

Finally, I have reached the shore. But I'm too late. Just when the sea swallows the large vessel, I get one final look at its name. Titanic III.

"And then my own screams woke me up."

Helmut sat at the bar. Opposite him, Marguerite

nodded understandingly and mixed his cocktail.

Syphilis. His brothers, his sisters. Dead at sea. Murdered. *Find the Centaur.*

"That sounds heavy, darling."

Marguerite's voice sounded comforting and safe.

Lonely child. Elitist parents. Rebel. No contact with next of kin.

"What do you think it means?"

Marguerite gently laughed and handed the cocktail to Helmut.

"It just sounds like a bad dream, doesn't it? I've never heard about the Titanic III."

"And neither do I have any friends called Syphilis."

"Then it's probably just that. A bad dream after a hard day at work. Or well, in your case, a night spent at a strip club stalking me."

I don't have any friends.

"Probably. But it all seemed so familiar."

"That's the beauty of dreams, isn't it? There's no boundaries in our dreams, only those we set ourselves. I have always envied people who have such vivid dreams."

"How so? Have you never dreamt?"

"My kind can't have dreams. It's the one thing our scientists never figured out. We live, but we don't dream."

"Has anyone ever figured out why that is?"

"No, otherwise we would have solved it a long time ago, darling."

Helmut grinned.

Darling.

"Anyway, I hope you're gonna feel better soon. That cocktail will definitely help with that."

"Promise?"

"Promise."

Categorically stunning.

Marguerite endearingly tapped her hoof onto Helmut's hybrid-skinned arm.

Helmut felt his electronics jump for a second. Being here did make him feel a lot better. He carefully took a sip from the orange cocktail in his hand.

Bitter.

A fitting start to the day.

"Liar!", he exclaimed. "It doesn't taste like a good start to the day at all."

He downed the rest of the cocktail anyway.

"Guess that makes me a liar then."

"Guess it does," Helmut smiled.

"For something that doesn't taste like a good start to the day, you seem pretty thirsty."

"I'm not planning to have a good day, Marguerite."

They both felt that joy had immediately left his voice.

"And how's that?" she asked while mixing a second cocktail.

"I'm attending Luciano's funeral."

"Oh, I didn't know you knew him."

"I didn't."

Marguerite stopped moving and stood still for a second.

Narrow, peerie eyes. Weight shifted to the rear legs. Chest pushed forward. Turgid udders. Explanation required.

Helmut quickly considered lying, then decided against it. There was something about her that made him want to tell her the truth. At least partly.

Trusting.

"I'm investigating his case."

He was uncertain as to what was happening here, but he trusted his instincts. Just like Syphilis had urged him to do.

"Investigating? I thought he committed suicide?"

"He did, technically. We're investigating what led to his suicide."

Marguerite nodded slowly.

"That sounds reasonable."

"That's my job, anyhow."

Helmut ran his hands through his dark hair. He still hadn't recovered from the intensity of his dream, let alone what it had transmitted.

"We wouldn't want any other suicides around here, would we?"

Marguerite's voice brought him back into reality, into the here and now. He smiled wickedly.

"Absolutely not. One is enough. Two would be plenty. Three is an epiphany."

Marguerite laughed out loud.

"Three is an epiphany. I've never heard that before. Has anyone ever told you how funny you are, Helmut?"

"Sarcasm is part of my DNA."

If only she knew how accurate that was. That all he consisted of was code and metal.

"Certainly seems that way, darling. For a human, you're pretty funny. Another one?"

He wanted to tell her, wanted to tell her the truth about himself, but he couldn't, not yet anyhow. Maybe in some distant future.

She pointed to the empty glass in his hand. Helmut nodded, and Marguerite began to mix his third of the day.

"Who says I'm not a hyper-secret robot you've never heard about?"

"Robots ain't funny. And robots don't drink the way you did last night."

"Maybe I'm more advanced than any of them?"

"So, you're special then?", she teased gently.

"The specialest", Helmut dryly replied, unwittingly copying Susan's grammar structure.

"Who knows, nobody ever catches the truth right in

front of them."

"Indeed, maybe I'm a highly advanced robot designed to become an alcoholic."

The thought of that conjured a smile on Marguerite's lips.

"Well, here's a special cocktail for a special hybrid then."

Helmut looked at her alarmed, but she had already turned around and didn't seem to think twice about what she just said. So close to the truth, it almost hurt. Helmut pinched his eyes.

"Thanks, Marguerite."

"I've never heard of anyone wanting to be a robot."

She shook her head in amusement.

"You're odd, Helmut. Really odd. I like it."

Helmut brought the glass to his lips to take another sip of his third cocktail of the day. Then it hit him with brute force like a tsunami clashing with the beach.

Nobody ever catches the truth right in front of them.

"How was I so blind? How the fuck was I so blind?"

Helmut's voice went head over heels when he realised the trajectory of his train of thought.

"What now?"

"You're brilliant, Marguerite. Absolutely brilliant. I could kiss you right now."

She laughed a bright laugh and shook her head.

"You really are odd, aren't you?"

Helmut downed his cocktail.

"I gotta go. You're a lifesaver. Quite literally."

He jumped up and ran towards the door, leaving a stunned and somewhat speechless Marguerite behind. Who was that guy?

Chapter Ten

The Funeral

Thousands of cows had come. The cemetery was too small to fit all of them, let alone all the other citizens of Paradise walking between old graves from the Last War marked with a white cross on top of them. All of Paradise was united in diversity, even the foxes had sent an ambassador to be present. Helmut hastily walked through the throngs of people in his way. Energy rays powered through him, and he could barely hide his excitement. Finally. This was what he was born to do. He had forgotten all about his dream and only focused on what was in front of him. Gently, but determined, he pushed through a group of donkeys who blocked half the road with their big rears, attempting to impress the nearby mares. Unsuccessful by all accounts. A not-so-rare smile manifested on Helmut's lips, and for a second, he envied them for their simplicity and illiteracy. A few stallions galloped across the streets, waving banners of all sorts, most commonly a mighty white tree in front of a dark blue background. Would Marguerite be here today? Most probably. Maybe if he looked out for her he could find her later. His eyes scanned the surroundings.

Cats lazily lay in the trees, dogs carried around vegan hot dogs on their backs and eagles flew high above in the sky, reporting to the bull regiment stationed to oversee today's funeral.

Too crowded. Hopeless.

Robots silently marched next to massive apes, and though the robots couldn't feel the cows' pain, nor did they understand their emotions, they were here to show their support on the orders of the Robot Councillor Timmothy for they knew it to be relevant to the cows. Then, through all the creatures, Helmut finally found whom he originally was looking for right in front of the entrance to the big hall where the ceremony would be held.

"Susan, I have a lead."

Susan turned around to him, a somewhat surprised look on her face. She tilted her head slightly, then raised a single eyebrow.

Expectant.

She didn't seem to endure a hangover after last night's shenanigans.

Odd.

"What? What is it? Tell me already."

"It's a message. It's been a message all along. We just didn't see it."

"Of course, it's a message, dumb dumb. That was our first idea. But we still haven't figured out what it means.

We know nothing."

"That's not it. We have been looking at this all wrong."

"What do you mean?"

"It's not so much about what the message might say but whom it is addressed to."

"I'm listening."

"Nobody knew I would be assigned to this. Neither did anyone know that you would be assigned to this case. We're random. But what wasn't random?"

"Stop playing games with me. Just tell me already," she demanded impatiently.

"Who has access to the information? Who sees everything we do?"

"You mean…?"

"Yes, I mean! The only one who gets all the information is Councillor Christine."

"I'm lost."

"Right, so was I until I met this wonderful epiphany of a cow who served me my drinks this morning. She's truly amazing. So great. Unbelievably brilliant. Mixes mean morning cocktails as well."

"Helmut, I get it. You're in love. Move on."

"I'm not. But anyway, the murder looked random, right? It might still be. But what wasn't random was who would oversee this investigation once it became obvious that a bull was murdered. I don't think the creature's origin was irrelevant. It was extraordinarily clear that most likely, the Councillor of the killed faction would oversee the investigation and have access to everything, including pictures and the projection of the carvings."

"So, why go to all the trouble of killing a bull when you could have just sent a picture or something like that? Why cause all of this?"

Susan widely gestured around to emphasise her point. It was certainly a spectacle.

"I don't know yet. I have absolutely no idea. But it's the only tangible connection that makes sense right now. If it was a message, then it needs a recipient. There was no way of knowing who would investigate, only who would oversee the investigation. That's all I know right now."

"Well, I'm not sold, I'm not gonna lie about that."

Susan tilted her head slightly to the left. But she didn't raise her eyebrow this time. *Scepticism.*

"But given that we don't have any other lead whatsoever, we might as well consider your wild theory."

Helmut grinned wickedly. He found himself doing that often recently, much to his own surprise.

"Why are you smiling? This isn't something to smile about."

"Oh, the game is on. Finally, something we can investigate. We have a murder on our hands. A mystery murder, Susan. Tell me that's not what you always dreamt about when your mother made you play with dumb dolls and sent you to ballet dances."

Susan rolled her eyes. "Fine. I might be a little excited. But just a little."

"You're a bad girl, aye."

Susan laughed inappropriately.

"The most bad."

Wrong tense. Answer to an inappropriate comment. Sarcasm.

"Good. There's a lot of work to be done."

"What's our next step?"

"Nobody can know about this. Not even the First Councillor."

"Why would I tell him in the first place, even if I had access to him? Councillor Christine oversees this investigation."

Helmut grabbed her arm. It felt oddly cold.

"Listen, Susan. I know why you're here. He sent you to spy on the investigation. That's why I was so mean in the beginning. And that's why we went for drinks. So I could evaluate you. I'm sorry."

While speaking those empty words, Helmut realised they weren't hollow at all. He meant them.

Very surprising. Run check.

Susan sighed loudly and seemed to weigh her options. Then she came to a decision and puckered her lips playfully and yet unknowingly.

Trusting.

"I did ignore you wonderfully, haven't I?"

Now it was Helmut's turn to roll his eyes.

"Nobody can know about this. Not the First Councillor, not Councillor Christine."

"Well, that'll be difficult. She's coming up to us. Right behind you."

Helmut let go of Susan's arm and turned around.

"Not a single word," he whispered without moving his lips.

Susan nodded and welcomed the Councillor with a lazy yet perfectly executed salute.

Military background, well hidden.

"Ah, my two detectives. Ready for the funeral?"

"Absolutely, Madame."

"Excellent. You two are gonna sit right behind me."

Councillor Christine was flanked by her two bodyguarding cows. Helmut greetingly nodded at them. He had seen them before. As always, they didn't respond.

Bloody cows.

"What is that? That smell? Has anyone here been drinking? This early in the morning?"

"I wouldn't know the first thing about it, Councillor Christine. I don't drink."

Helmut accusingly turned around to Susan, a single

eyebrow raised.

"Interesting," Councillor Christine murmured and looked at Susan disapprovingly before moving towards her assigned seat in the big hall.

"I can't believe you just did that," Susan whispered.

Deadly stare.

If only stares could kill.

"We're here today to honour Luciano Franculo. Many of you knew him, others heard about him, all of you are here to pay your respects to him. While Luciano was many things, he was first and foremost an idealist who believed in Paradise. Who loved his friends and family, who, many of you have told me, one could always rely on and who one could always have a good time with. And so, I believe, and I hope we can all agree on this, Luciano will be happy to see all of us here today. Not just to honour his memory, but because everyone came, no matter whether they knew him or not, whether they had heard about him before or not, and no matter whether robot or human, dog, cat, horse or donkey, eagle, ape or cow. We're all here. United in diversity. Just as he preached. Just as he believed in. And yet, I've been told that his strong beliefs sometimes caused discussions and arguments, especially his favourite topic, Sig's Canal. Luciano, it is said, was a strong advocate to re-open Paradise's borders to all those who have not had the privilege to be born and raised in Paradise. Not many agreed with him, in fact, his family told me, nobody ever really did. Yet, he would not waver in his beliefs, and he would not fail to stand up for what he believed could be a better world. And while it wasn't always easy, it was still beautiful to watch Luciano being so passionate and loving that he wanted to extend his love to all, those he didn't even know about or whether they existed at all. Dear family, dear friends, I want you always to remember this about Luciano, he…"

At that moment, someone explosively charged through the door. In the blink of an eye, Helmut turned around, pointing a Glock 19 in the door's direction, ready to shoot.

A charging cow. Civilian. No weapon. Eyes widened. Panicked. No immediate danger. Store weapon into holster.

Loud whispers ran through the crowd like bullets passing through soldiers' chests.

"Volker, what's the meaning of this?"

Councillor Christine had also jumped out of her chair, standing on all fours, ready to charge the invader. Her eyes had become a furious red which Helmut had never seen before in his short life. Her voice a sharp sword cutting through the incipient murmurs like metal through bones.

"Councillor Christine. There's… we found… there."

"Calm down, Volker. Take a big breath. What's going on?"

"They found a second body, Councillor Christine."

Then, exhausted, Volker sank to the floor.

For a moment, it was deadly silent in the hall, and one could have heard a pin drop on the marble floor.

Widening eyes. Slightly opened mouths. Jerky movements. Panic imminent. Chaos erupting shortly.

"Susan, I hope you remember your spec ops training. It'll get ugly any second now."

Susan already stood next to him, ready to reach for her weapon. She didn't even deny her military past, just nodded.

"Councillor, with me. We're getting you out of here. Just in case. Susan, cover us. Concealed. Bodyguard cows. Make yourself useful for once and keep the others at bay. Nobody likes you, anyway."

Helmut took the fraction of a second to thank his creators for his inner calmness, then he pushed the Councillor towards the back exit. Behind him, chaos erupted.

Chapter Eleven

The Ambassador

Muscles showing underneath the short hide. Gentle movements. Loud cheering. A smile so sharp it could have cut Helmut in half. Spoken words so wicked that Helmut winced slightly at the memory of it. Eyes so wondrous, he lost himself in them as in a vast ocean without shores.

"Helmut, are you listening? Hey!"

Susan's stern voice reactivated his senses with a jerk, and he focused on his surroundings.

"Sorry. My bad. What did you just say?"

"I said, the entire City is on lockdown. Nobody is allowed out after curfew."

"That's a huge mistake."

"I know, but the Council has spoken. We're under lockdown. The police robots are on patrol, eagles provide overwatch and cow cavalry circles around the City's borders to prevent anyone from leaving or entering."

Helmut stretched his shoulders.

"As is protocol, I assume."

"As is protocol indeed. Only, this specific protocol hasn't been enacted since the end of the Last War."

Helmut and Susan were about to pass by two massive apes standing guard in front of the Embassy. They wore their longswords across their backs, making them look even more significant than they were already while holding lances in their hands. Helmut nodded towards them in greeting. Icy eyes followed his movements. These apes were the strongest warriors there were, their thick skin making it almost impossible to penetrate them with common bullets.

Not welcomed here. Mercenary apes. Careful.

The entire Embassy was on alert after the lockdown. The two bodyguarding cows followed Helmut and Susan dutifully as they had always done and would probably continue to do until either of them died. Which, given the current situation, was more likely than ever before. It wouldn't be much of a loss.

The apes locked their lances in front of the entrance.

"You shall not pass," one of them declared in a deep voice.

"My name is Helmut. This is Susan. We've been invited by the Ambassador herself."

"You may pass."

Easy.

The two apes unlocked their lances and opened the way for the four creatures in front of them. When Helmut and Susan passed through, a wicked smile appeared on her lips.

"We've been invited, but not those two," she whispered gently into the ape's ear.

His eyes hardened, and with a sweeping motion, their lances pointed towards the two bodyguarding cows who helplessly watched Helmut and Susan disappear into the Embassy. One of the few remaining ones. Helmut waved his hands in a silent, almost regretful goodbye. Almost.

"That was fun," Susan giggled.

Helmut chuckled approvingly.

Re-assessment. Potential asset.

"I figured, given our newest working theory, it might be wise to get rid of the two, and since you didn't seem to be able to shake them off…"

"I get it, Susan. Smart play. No need to ruin your moment."

Helmut's voice sounded cold, but his eyes gave away his amusement.

"Ah, the famous detectives nobody seems to know about. Welcome to the Embassy of the Independent State of California."

"Ms Ambassador, it is an honour to meet you."

Helmut bowed in front of the mighty woman in front of him.

"No need for such formalities, we're in private."

"Of course, Ms Ambassador. As you wish."

No bullshit. Equal players.

"Come now. I'd like to show you the reason why

you're here. It's quite entertaining."

The Ambassador led Helmut and Susan up the stairs into a vast conference room. With a gentle motion of her hand, she lowered an extensive monitor on the other side of the room.

"Please. Make yourself comfortable. The show is about to start. It's intriguing, I promise."

"Ms Ambassador, with all due respect. I don't think we have the time to watch a movie. We were just on our way to…"

"Oh, Susan. I know. You were just on your way to the second murder scene nobody is supposed to know about."

Investigation has been infiltrated. Proceed with caution.

For the first time since Helmut met Susan, she seemed speechless.

"How…?"

"How do I know? You're not the only ones acting behind people's backs, hiding in the shadows, ready to strike the moment you're ordered to. We're all operating in Paradise, honey. We're all snakes offering the apple to the innocent, only nobody quite seems to know who has taken a bite from the forbidden fruit which is the dead bull on our hands. Well, on your hands, really. The State of California has her own bloody war to fight overseas. I heard you're about to dispatch your Foreign Legion though. Very generous."

Reassessment. Insider information. Proceed with caution.

"I'm afraid we can neither deny nor confirm that."

"Enough with the chitchat. I'm not here to expose your investigation, and neither do I want to waste your time. I thought I'd share a few details with you which would probably be hard for you to come by otherwise."

"That is very generous of you, Ms Ambassador," Helmut expressed while trying to keep his composure.

The Ambassador made him nervous. There was a game being played right in front of him which he couldn't quite place.

Insufficient information. Reassessment.

"Now, before we watch this little clip together, I need your assurance that this stays between the three of us. It is of utmost importance to my government that nobody knows about this."

"With all due respect, Ms Ambassador, you know we cannot give you such a promise."

"Well shit," she exhaled. "Then you might as well leave now because I won't share my information with you then."

"Yes, you will," Susan quietly whispered just loud enough for the three to hear it.

Even though it was utterly silent in the conference room, Susan spoke with a quiet intensity that Helmut had never heard before.

"Oh, will I now?"

The Ambassador seemed amused and ran her fingers through her hair. Her long fingernails got stuck.

Nervous. Well hidden.

"Indeed," Helmut supported Susan.

"And why is that?"

"Because, whatever you're about to show us, you don't feel you can share it with Paradise's Diplomatic Corps as would be protocol. We're here because you need something. Something unofficial from someone acting in the shadows, and for some reason, we're the ones you've chosen."

"Assuming that is the case, do we have a deal?"

"That vastly depends on the information you're about to provide us with," Helmut asserted.

"Fair enough. Here's my offer. I will share two pieces of information with you. The first is a short video of our security cameras. The second is a secret for now, but I promise you that it'll be worth it."

"Why would we be interested in what your security cameras recorded?"

"Because it shows the second murdered creature minutes before his end."

Assessment: true.

Helmut shared a look with Susan and covertly nodded his head.

"What do you want in return?"

"The creature stole something from us. Something important to my government. You'll recover it, bring it to me, and won't tell a living soul on this planet about it."

"What is it that was stolen?"

"I'm not at liberty to say, I'm afraid."

Helmut laughed.

"How on earth are we supposed to find something when we don't even know what we're looking for?"

"You will know when you find it, don't worry. It'll all become obvious at the end."

Assessment: true.

"You're speaking in riddles."

"Our entire existence is one big, messy riddle. Why not add a second, slightly less intriguing riddle to the equation?"

"Because none of this matters if we can't solve the riddle of our existence."

"Wrong. If nothing matters, then only the things we assign value to matter. And it happens to be the case that the stolen item has assigned value for me. Just as solving the criminal case has value for you, I would assume."

"So, do we have a deal?"

Helmut questioningly checked with Susan. She nodded her head slightly, though she seemed less than convinced that this was a good idea.

"You have a deal, Ms Ambassador."

"Excellent, showtime."

Slight exhale. Relieved.

The Ambassador waved her hand, and the screen turned on.

An empty room. Desks, Chairs, Shelves. Probably an office. The sunflower Californian flag behind the desk, an old bust standing proudly in the left corner. Authoritative figure. Silence. A fox enters through the window, his hide painted a dark black. He's barely visible against the background. He walks upright towards the desk. Appears to know the office. Seemingly effortless, he opens the desk's top drawer, quickly unlocks the integral safe and takes something out of it to store it in his backpack.

Cannot identify the object. Blocked by the desk. Before the fox can leave through the window, an ape walks into the office. In the fraction of a second, the fox jumps towards the ape, holding a previously hidden blade. With a familiar gesture, he cuts the ape's throat with one blow. The ape falls down, surprise showing on his face. He presses both hands against his throat, but the blood continues to pour out of the large wound that looks like a wild grin on somebody's face. Without looking back once, the fox jumps out of the window.

The screen turned black, and it took Helmut and Susan a second to understand that the clip had ended.

"What the actual fuck," Susan exhaled.

"What happened to the ape?" Helmut asked, seemingly recovering his composure instantly.

"She died. Bled out on the floor. It's a pity, really. That carpet was brand new. Ruined."

The Ambassador's cold voice said more than a thousand words ever could. Whatever the fox had stolen meant a lot more than the life of a mere ape, or any creature, it appeared.

"Well then. We better get to work. Thank you for sharing this with us, Ms Ambassador. I'm certain it will be most useful to our investigation."

"No, it won't," she laughed. "But hopefully it will be helpful to my interests."

The Ambassador ushered Helmut and Susan towards the door. Though not in shock from what they had just seen, they were seemingly surprised by recent events.

"Oh, one last thing, Helmut. Before I forget. Not everyone appears to be who you think they are. The person you're looking for. The murderers. They go by the name of 'The Centaur'. Some of our operatives clashed with them in the City of Spies a while back. They're the real deal. Dangerous. Tread lightly if you want to survive, the both of you. I'd love to provide you with more information but I'm afraid I don't have any other than their operational space in the City of Spies. Take this, you'll find it useful. An old friend gave it to me a long time ago."

She pressed a dark envelope into Helmut's hand and winked at him.

Epilogue

Dawn

The cave was empty and dark. Too dark to see anything. Yet, Pamé walked through the sheer nothingness of the hollow cave as if it was well-lit. She misplaced not a single step, did not halt once, did not hesitate for a second. If there had been light, the creatures following her would have seen a tall woman with sinning, ever-seeing eyes. But, of course, there was no light. The creatures didn't need any to recognise their surroundings, and neither did Pamé. She had seen this place too many times, memorised its paths and knew all the little pitfalls in her way. She moved with the gentle, idle wisdom of age-old power.

Pamé and her envoys continued to walk through the darkness until she recognised the tiniest of lights in front of her. It was only a dim, almost unnoticeable change in the nothingness around her, but for her sharp eyes, it was as if lightning had struck. Suddenly, she recognised her surroundings instead of merely knowing them. She walked around the corner where her brother had fallen, passed by the spot where she had first seen the Kaiserpaar, and arrived at the massive lake in the middle of the cave where the first hybrid had been created. Once upon a time, history had been made here, but it was long forgotten, their memories had fallen to the tooth of time, and only her distant dreams brought them back to life every now and then.

Pamé stopped in front of the lake. Light seemingly coming from nowhere reflected on the water, mirrored the cave's ceiling. Behind her, the envoys took position. She turned around to them and gave each of the three creatures a gentle smile.

"Thank you, Captain, for bringing me this far. I release you from your duty to me. This next step of our journey is not meant for you."

"Commander, with all due respect, we won't be released. We swore to follow, serve and protect you until death releases us. We'll wait for you right here."

Pamé recognised the determination in his voice. Once a loyal soldier, always a loyal soldier.

"As you wish. Wait here for our return."

The robots nodded and took a step back, giving way for a young woman.

"Is this where it all happened?"

Pamé nodded.

"This is the place. Our first hybrids were created here. The Kaiserpaar guided their rebellion from here. The Prophecy has been foretold here."

She turned around to the young woman.

"I never dared to believe this place truly existed. All

the legends, all the myths about it but my research never found any feasible evidence for this place."

Pamé touched the scar on her right cheek absentmindedly.

"It wouldn't be much of a secret if everyone could simply walk into here."

"But Paradise's library. All the knowledge of the remaining world is said to be stored in there and I couldn't find anything. Not a single shred of evidence this place existed."

"Of course not. My organisation made sure of that. We're only safe as long as nobody knows about us. Otherwise, hell will reign once more on Earth."

"But nothing at all? Even if your organisation was the most thorough on Earth, and I don't doubt you are, even then, there must have been something."

"Oh, but there is. There are clues for those who know how to find them. They're just not in the obvious places, my dear."

A disappointed look covered the young woman's face.

"That's not my fault," she said defensively.

"Of course not," Pamé laughed. "They weren't meant for you."

The young woman rolled her eyes.

"You never tell me anything."

"I'll do you one better. I'll show you. Come on. We've got work to do."

Without another word, Pamé turned around and jumped into the water. She swam to the middle of the lake, where she waited for the young woman to catch up with her. The sound of moving water resounded through the cave. Pamé felt the cold water eat through her thermo-suit. It was colder than the last time that she had been here.

“What now?”

“Now, you’ll learn the truth behind the fairytales they taught you in Paradise.”

“How?”

“Follow me. Stay right behind me. Don’t lose touch or you may never make it back.”

Pamé took a deep breath, then another, and another. Then, finally, she dove deep into the waters. Further down than most people could. Even further than most people dared. The absorbed air began to leave her, she felt her muscles tire without the oxygen, felt the coldness tear on her skin. Just when she was ready to open her mouth and drink all the water around her in an attempt to take a regular breath, just when her chest tightened and unspeakable pain overcame her, she felt the opening above her. She catapulted herself towards it, and couldn’t have been without air for a second longer when she finally reached it. Beside her, the young woman desperately gasped for air. They lay still there for a few minutes, doing nothing but taking deep breaths and relaxing their tight muscles. When Pamé finally rolled over and jumped up like a cat, she was breathing normally again.

"Welcome to the Alliance's graveyard."

They stood in a vast hole of sorts, somehow breathing fresh air. The young woman's eyes searched her surroundings for the origin of it, but before she found anything, something else caught her attention. The original Prophecy, the first written testament of its existence.

She had long been searching for any evidence, not knowing whether it truly existed or was a mere fairytale. But here she was, far away from Paradise, and by a mere accident had finally found the truth behind the legends.

When Europe has become a paradise
Then there are no more parasites
When light has triumphed over darkness
Then there is no more apartness

When all live in togetherness
Then we shall rise for the first time
When all are touched by gentleness
Then we shall return the crime

When the darkest of hours
Follows the brightest of hours

When he who is promised
Returns for all is lawless

And when he who is promised
Roams paradise's streets again
We shall rise to the throne
Walking over those who used to own

When the young woman finally broke free from the engraved wall, her eyes were wide and scared.

"This is different. I've seen translations of it. They sound nothing like it."

"No, of course not. Nobody inside Paradise is allowed to know its true content. It would cause upheaval if anyone ever actually truly knew what it was about."

"So we've been fed a lie all of our lives? Not that it matters. It's all there now."

Pamé nodded.

"It's always been right here where nobody dared to look."

"Is that why the Council is sending expeditions across the Canal?"

"No, it's not. They're searching for something else entirely. They're looking for lifeforms, not long-forgotten people."

"But surely they must know about the Prophecy?"

"Oh, they do. But they believe the same fairytale the

cows have given all of Paradise. That it was their Oracle, who proclaimed the one who is promised. The same legend you believed until recently, if I'm correct."

A rueful smile covered the young woman's face.

"Guilty as charged. But you must admit, it's lucky that the Council has never found this place."

"Of course. We can count ourselves lucky that they haven't yet discovered this cave, but I would bet my left testicle, if only I had one, that the cows are doing everything in their power to stop future expeditions."

The young woman nodded thoughtfully and read over the Prophecy again.

"What do you think of it?" Pamé asked.

"It's frightening. It's frightening me. I always thought Paradise would survive and provide us with peace. Now I don't know what to think anymore. And there's something else, I just don't quite know how to phrase it in words yet."

"We've all been there, darling. It's not easy to comprehend."

"We have to stop them."

"We will."

"How do we start?"

"We have long started. That's why you're here. It was no mere accident that we found you."

The young woman nodded understandingly.

"What can I do to help?"

Pamé smiled.

"Your presence with us is all we need for now. Train with us, familiarise yourself with our traditions, prepare for what is yet to come."

"Is there anything else?"

"There's just one final thing I have to do."

Pamé kneeled in front of one of the three stone coffins, resting one of her hands on the engraved face. For a moment there, it seemed almost as if she was praying, but the young woman knew her better than that. She couldn't understand Pamé's broken voice, but she recognised her meaning regardless. When Pamé stood up, a single tear ran down her cheek. Her eyes were cold then and had lost all colour, a dark vortex which absorbed everything around her.

Part II - The Dead Fox

Prologue

The Beginning

The sun was just setting on the horizon when the mid-sized cow walked into the large office on the top floor of the new Timcorps Enterprises HQ. Her long legs elegantly moved in a slow rhythm, almost too slow for the eye to really catch it. It looked almost as if she wasn't moving at all, were it not for the soft but determined clacking of her cow shoes on the wooden floor. The orange light of the sunset gently brightened the expansive room, reflecting softly in the glass and metal all around the cow. A man sat on one of the alligator leather couches and seemed to stare right into the disappearing sun, like Newton once did. His full head of hair stood wildly in all directions and would have given him a comical look if it wasn't for his eyes. They were like a dark vortex, absorbing everything around him. Ever-looking, ever-searching, ever-hunting.

"Ah, Christine. Welcome. I've been waiting for you."

"I could imagine you'd have better things to do than wait for a lonely assistant to the Cow Councillor."

"I could imagine that would be the case if she wasn't like a sister to me."

The man grinned and hugged Christine. It was a tight

hug. The sort of hug that only came after years of knowing one another. It was the embrace of everything they meant to each other. It was something else entirely.

"Corpsi, it's good to see you again. It's been too long."

Not many people knew about his nickname, and even fewer dared to use it. Christine had been the one to introduce it years ago when they met during their respective internships at Paradise's embassy to Fox Nation.

"I'm afraid it has been," Corps agreed and gestured to one of the couches.

Christine took a seat and relaxed. She had grown out her hide since they last met a few months ago and painted her hooves in an elegant and intriguing navy blue. Her long hide curled slightly in all the right places. She could tell that none of this remained unnoticed by Corps. His eyes were constantly moving, never staying still, almost as if they were looking for something else entirely, which even he himself didn't know about.

"Want some wine? We recently discovered a winery near the remains of Bordeaux. It's a good year."

"Which year is it?" Christine asked curiously.

Old wine was something of a rarity these days. Most of it had been contaminated one way or another and even though some of the expertise of making wine had survived the Last War, a lot had gone missing. The

French were particularly secretive about it these days.

"It's my favourite year: 2020."

Christine laughed.

"Well, if I remember my history lessons correctly, that wine is probably the only good thing that happened that year. Those poor creatures back then."

"Au contraire," Corps grinned. "I have it on good account that a lot went right in his life that year."

"Are you still reading the diaries you found?"

He smiled gently.

"I am. Much better entertainment than what our industries produce these days. So much more heart-breaking, so desperate, so enlightening."

Christine couldn't help herself but laugh.

"You and your flair for the dramatic…"

"Excuse me, that poor soul still didn't tell her that he's desperately in love with her. Instead, he goes on and on about her. It's like a never-ending story. If even one-quarter of what he claims about her is true, she must have been more beautiful than Cleopatra, smarter than Einstein, more wicked than Lucifer and scarier than an angel of death."

"Have you ever met an angel of death?"

Corps grinned and swallowed some wine.

"Only you."

He said it so matter-of-factly that for a short moment, Christine almost felt elevated. Almost.

She tried the wine and a satisfied sigh left her lips.
"You're right. This is truly excellent."
"Good. We have plenty of it."

For the next few hours, they forgot the world around them and talked. Just talked like they hadn't done in forever. Though they were both critical creatures in the greater framework of Paradise, there was nothing quite like two old friends catching up. Just when Christine forgot that Corps wasn't the sentimental type, all his laughter fell off him like a wet cloak in front of a hot fireplace. She could feel the change in his attitude immediately, though he made no attempt to hide it. Had his eyes been bright and beautiful before, resting entirely on her, they had suddenly begun to stare right into her soul as if they were searching for the answer to a question he hadn't asked yet.

"What is it?" she asked him carefully.

She knew she had to tread lightly. He was easily spooked.

"What I'm about to tell you can never leave this room. Ever."

"You know nothing you tell me will ever be known to another soul."

He remained silent.

"I promise," Christine added.

He shook his head.

"That's not good enough. I need you to swear to it."

She resisted the temptation to roll her eyes. He did have a flair for the dramatic.

"I swear."

"Swear it on the Oracle herself."

All easiness left Christine. This was serious. Though not many people believed in the Oracle these days, Corps knew that she did. Swearing on her name was the most considerable promise anyone could ever ask of her.

"I swear on the Oracle herself that nothing you tell me today, will tell me, or ever told me will be known by another soul."

Content, he relaxed and slightly shifted in his seat. Then, he took a deep breath.

"I need to send an expedition across the Canal."

There was no doubt in his voice, only determination.

"The First Councillor Thommy has expressly forbidden any further expeditions across the Canal. Paradise will continue to protect its borders but not expand that protection beyond the Canal."

"I'm well aware of this administration's foolishness", he said bitterly.

"It's unknown terrain. The barbarians out there are dangerous. We aren't yet strong enough to push them from the continent."

"What do you think?"

"I agree with the honourable Councillor."

"Bullshit, you don't."

Christine's eyes wandered uneasily through the office.

"There are no cameras here, no microphones. It's just us."

Christine hadn't expected anything less. Corps had always been a bit paranoid.

"Why do you want to cross the Canal?" she deflected.

"I believe that Visila is still alive."

The words stood silently in the room, stood between Corps and Christine.

"That's impossible," Christine exhaled in disbelief.

"She's alive," he stated firmly.

She recognised that he wouldn't back down on this. His fiery eyes gave him away.

"We saw her die," she said gently. "I understand your urge to believe she's alive, but we saw her die right in front of our eyes."

He shook his head.

"We didn't see her die. The sea swallowed her in front of us, but we never saw her die. Or found her body."

Christine bitterly laughed.

"She was lost in the middle of the Baltic Sea, right in the contaminated section where all the old nuclear submarines sunk during that joint military exercise."

"I know that she's not. I can sense it."

"You can sense it? Corpsi, I miss her as much as you do, but there's no way she could have survived."

He frowned.

"She's alive."

"Fine, even if she was alive, and even if she was beyond the Canal, the Council would never allow an expedition. It's too dangerous. There's no way around that. Our resources are too thin to risk such exposure. You know what's out there. Barbarians. Contaminated areas. Old bombs and explosives from the Last War. It's a wasteland out there. A deadly wasteland. Nobody ever came back."

"I think I may have found a way around that."

Christine leaned forward. She unconsciously gripped her glass tighter and it broke between her hooves.

Wine splattered all over the expensive carpets, but neither of the two creatures cared about it. They stared at each other the way a cobra eyes its next victim.

"How?"

"Robots."

She shook her head in disappointment. For a moment there his sheer will had almost convinced her of the possibility to explore and expand beyond Sig's Canal.

"We tried robots. Too many complications, too many problems. Our tech is not advanced enough."

"My robots will be."

"Your robots failed already."

Corps grinned wickedly.

"Not the newest generation. Not the Combrine Series.

Not these."

"I have never heard of them."

"They're new. Brand new. Still in the conception phase, but they will be the most advanced artificial creatures ever created. They will be real. They will be able to simulate emotions and act on them. They will look like humans, like cows, like eagles, you name it."

"So, what's the problem?"

"Technically, currently, they're illegal."

"You don't expect the design to be approved by the Council?"

"Not in its current composition, no. Besides, I wouldn't trust the Council with anything so precious."

Christine nodded slowly.

"So, you're proposing to build an illegal robot series to explore an area expressly forbidden by the Council in an attempt to find the dead Visila?"

Corps smiled. It wasn't the sinister smile Christine had expected of him. Not even a confident, daring one. Instead, it was a warm, gentle smile. An honest smile. The most honest she had seen him smile since Visila had died in that piracy attack on the Baltic Sea. At that moment, it struck Christine. He truly did believe Visila was still alive, after all this time. He truly did think he could find her and bring her back to him. It was a hopeful smile from a man who had lost all hope a long time ago.

"That's not all I'm proposing. Somebody needs to get the Council to grant me special freedoms for the Combrines."

Christine's mind immediately jumped to the endless opportunities and risks.

"Who are you thinking of bribing? Probably the donkeys and humans, maybe also the horses…"

"Nothing like that. It'd be too insecure, not permanent enough."

"What else do you have in mind?"

"We replace the current Cow Councillor. She's the leading voice against my plans. Without her, nobody will dare block our vision. Why the fuck does she hate technological progress so much?"

"That's a dangerous thought."

"It's the only thought that matters."

"Who do you want to replace her with?"

Corps smiled. This time, it was the sinister smile Christine had grown to love on his face. Then, in the middle of the growing silence, he expectantly raised a single, perfectly plucked eyebrow.

Casually, Christine leaned back into her seat. Too casually. Before any actual words had left her thoughtful lips, both of them knew what her answer would be.

Chapter One

The Second Body

"Well, it'll be difficult to hide this one."

"My COCC isn't going to be amused."

A shy smile appeared on Susan's lips.

"Your COCC is never amused."

"Aren't you a smartie today," Helmut chuckled.

Eagles circled over them and police robots had built a makeshift circle around the body, trying to prevent the oncoming crowd from gathering more than a few glimpses of the dead fox. Despite the instantly imposed lockdown, hundreds of creatures stood around the crime scene. Cavalry cows gently, but determinedly, pushed the crowd further back. For an occasion such as this, it all took place rather quietly and peacefully. In fact, the silence struck Helmut as odd. It was awfully silent. There were a few murmurs from the crowd, paired with the intent and metallic steps of the cows' hooves. Then, there were the almost unnoticeable mechanical movements of the robots, the soft vibrations in the air which the flying eagles caused and then, there was Susan. Her bright laugh seemed awfully misplaced, cutting through the silence like the French Guillotine through necks, her sparkling eyes not even attempting to hide her amusement over the situation. Dogs and cats turned around to the laughing creature, eyeing her suspiciously. The horses in the crowd tried to use the advantage of their height to see over the robots but were hindered by their ever-stalking donkey admirers. As always, there were no foxes to be seen. Except one. He silently lay in a pool of wet blood on the floor of a vast park within the City.

Déjà vu.

"I've never seen a prettier fox, to be honest."

They stood over a tiny dead body, his hide painted a deep black, even more intense than in the video shown by the Ambassador. If Helmut hadn't seen it with his own eyes, he wouldn't have believed that this tiny creature had slain a mercenary ape just before his own demise.

"I kinda like his style. The black pairs wonderfully with the hole in his forehead."

"You're right, and the still-wet blood adds superbly to the leaking brain all over the place."

"It's a piece of art, indeed."

"The only thing that's missing from this masterpiece is the one thing we came for…"

"Ironically, we don't even know what we're looking for, but we know that it's missing."

"Well, that's just life, isn't it?"

"You must have lived a sad life, Helmut."

Susan flashed a cheeky smile.

"On a more serious note, are you as confused as I am about the whole Ambassador shenanigans?"

"The whole snake offering the forbidden fruit bit felt a bit surreal. For all I know the bible has been banned from Paradise a long time ago."

"She does have a thing for the overdramatic, it seems."

"And yet it appears that we struck a deal with the devil."

"Yeah, about that. We might need another night in the bar to debate the latest development in private. It seems we find ourselves in quite the pickle..."

Susan shared another inappropriate laugh which earned her confused looks by the robots. Even they knew that it was not proper to laugh at this moment. Their code told them not to, though, of course, they didn't quite understand why. Or even question their orders, for that matter.

Susan's loud laugh appeared to have awoken the nearby birds hiding in the park's trees. Almost as if they responded to Susan's reaction to the killed fox, they began to sing. Slow and quiet at first as if they weren't quite sure whether they were allowed to fill the silence with bristling sounds. But then, after a few long seconds, their cackling and quacking, singing and shrieking began, almost as if they gossiped, chatting about the news of a second dead creature in Paradise. An astonishing story, indeed. It seemed only right for the birds to tell the world about this murder, now that even a foreign power seemed to know more about the inner workings of Paradise than its citizens. But they were mere birds, not members of the Great Nine. Nobody would entirely listen to the birds and their loud singing, and even if anyone did listen, nobody would be able to understand what they were saying. They hadn't learned to speak the proper tongue yet, and for all Helmut knew, they never would.

Thus was their destiny; knowledgeable but unable to communicate.

"Do you ever pity robots?"

"Why would I?" Helmut asked back, painfully aware of the irony behind that.

"Because they don't get this humour, or any sort of humour really. They don't get why we're laughing about this."

"By that definition, I'd have to pity most of the Great Nine."

"Wicked as always, my dear Helmut. Wicked as always."

"I do have my moments."

"More often than not, I'm afraid."

A police robot approached Helmut and Susan. He too seemed perplexed about the easy laughter the two shared while standing over the massacred fox's body, carefully avoiding the pool of wet blood and brain.

"Sir and Madame, I'm Robot 950302. I was the first at the scene. I'm here to share the preliminary report."

"Do share it, Robot 950302."

"The dead body has been identified as a fox, it is yet unknown who he is or why he was here. We have approached the Fox Embassy for clarification, but so far they haven't responded to our request. The fox appears to have been shot in the head from a close distance. We have found and identified the bullet. It's standard ammunition, 9 mm. There's no CCTV footage in the park. The screening of surrounding cameras has not produced any suspects. Not a single one."

"That's everything?"

"Yes, Madame. We will provide the relevant department with the full report once it has been concluded."

"You will do no such thing, Robot 950302. On orders of Councillor Christine herself, you will report directly to her office and nobody else. Am I understood?"

"Sir, I have received detailed instructions by the Council."

"I'm declaring this case directly connected to the Fallen Bull, which, surprise surprise, is my investigation. It's been tagged. Check with your supervisors if you must, but unless you want to be deactivated, I'd do as I tell you. Understood?"

"Understood, Sir."

Without another word, the robot turned around and left Helmut and Susan behind.

"That was a little harsh, wasn't it?"

"I'm just saving us the trouble to explain to the Councillor why this investigation hasn't been assigned to her office directly. Besides, it's just a bloody robot. Robots don't feel. By definition, he cannot be hurt. It's a beautiful world we're living in, don't you think?"

Susan gently rolled her eyes as she often did when Helmut opened his mouth.

"Humour me for a second, Helmut, but without knowing about our visit with the Ambassador, how exactly is this case linked to the Fallen Bull? As far as I can see, this is officially a killing whereas the bull was declared a suicide, there are no carvings here, but instead, we found a bullet and it's a fox which was killed, not a bull. Besides, isn't Councillor Christine, well, not necessarily a suspect but a person of interest in the Fallen Bull investigation?"

"It is odd, isn't it?"

"What exactly?"

"The most relevant things here are the ones that are missing."

"How so?"

"Let's start with the obvious. There are no carvings

here which we assumed was the entire reason to kill the Fallen Bull in the first place. Then, we know for a fact that the fox should be in possession of a certain item, but he isn't. Lastly, the absence of any CCTV footage isn't entirely suspicious at all."

"Right. I see where you're going with this. The lack of CCTV footage could mean that this was planned, and the close proximity from which the shot was taken suggests that the fox must have known his killer."

"Not only that. For all we know, this is a highly trained and specialised fox. He has just killed an ape. A bloody mercenary ape. Those things are hard to kill, let alone with a simple blade. So a highly trained, highly alerted fox lets someone come close enough to shoot him point-blank into the face. He must have trusted whoever did this a lot."

"Say that again, Helmut."

"What? He must have trusted his killer?"

"No, the other thing. The bladed thing."

"He killed the ape with a hidden blade, remember?"

"Of course, I do, Helmut. But where's the blade?" Susan exclaimed.

Helmut quickly re-analysed his surroundings.

No blade.

"Maybe he dropped it on his way here?"

"I doubt it. That fox was executing a precise mission and seemed to have no other weapon than that blade. I'd bet my life that he would have kept it."

"So then, the murderer must have taken it."

"But why? I get that the item was taken. That must have been the reason for this murder. But why take the blade as well?"

"Susan, this might surprise you, but I have absolutely no idea. No clue whatsoever."

"It doesn't surprise me at all."

And with that, her bright laugh returned. Helmut couldn't help himself but chuckle.

"So, in conclusion, we don't the fuck know what happened here?"

"It seems that way, indeed. Again."

"Well, there is one thing we know."

"And that is?"

Helmut showed Susan the envelope the Ambassador gave him.

"We know the Centaur killed the bull and probably this fox."

"Whoever that might be."

"It doesn't matter who he is. We must find him."

Susan sighed.

"I don't know about you, but I could use a drink."

"Agreed. Let me finish up here. Meet you at the usual bar in two hours?"

"It's a date," Helmut grinned.

"I doubt it."

"Me too."
"Don't bring your COCC."

Chapter Two

The Foxy

Heavy bass vibrations bounced off Helmut's hybrid skin, unbeknown to all those surrounding him, his robotic body stood in the bar like a rock in the surf, an odd island which the vibrations and sounds couldn't reach nor glide through. He was impossible to penetrate while the music tore figurative holes in the few other bodies in the bar. As always, the room was lit in a sensitive red, reminding him of something he couldn't quite place.

"Is Susan not coming today?"

Neshama snorted a line of jarringly pink powder through her human nose.

"Ah, that's the stuff," she continued, without awaiting Helmut's response.

"She's just running a bit late."

Neshama smiled and offered Helmut the powder.

"What is that even?"

"Some new stuff from Fox Nation. Their chemists are the best in the world, that is to say in Paradise. If their little island is still considered to be Paradise. I've never been great at geography."

Helmut laughed.

Unsurprising.

Neshama looked at him intensely through her hazelnut eyes and pulled him into her gaze. All of a sudden, he understood why Susan was so fond of Neshama. There was something about her even he found difficult to withstand. The way she moved reminded him of a cat and those eyes seemed to always search for prey to be hunted. They never stood still, never entirely focused on one thing, were never completely satisfied. Her eyes absorbed him like the early Roman Empire had absorbed the Italian tribes.

"Sure, I'll have a bite."

Without knowing why he just said that, Helmut took the offered powder and sorted it into a line. His hybrid-skinned nose exploded the moment he snorted it.

Highly addictive. Illegal. Releases endorphins. Advanced drug.

His systems quickly absorbed and filtered the powder to render its effects useless.

"Woah, that's quite the stuff, indeed."

"You'll be feeling it in no time, I promise you."

"What will he be feeling in no time?"

Energy levels spiking.

Helmut would have recognised that voice through a snowstorm.

Marguerite.

"The Foxy," Neshama laughed brightly, showing the first signs of her intake.

Helmut turned around to Marguerite who stood tall in front of him, her smile reaching her green eyes.

"I didn't take you for the drug-taking type, Helmut."

"I… I mean, I… usually, I don't."

What the fuck. Restart riposte folder.

Estimated time: 3 seconds.

Marguerite laughed an easy laugh and hugged Helmut.

"It's good seeing you again, Helmut."

"It's good seeing you again, too."

Restart completed.

"Well, it's good seeing the two of you," Neshama laughed.

"And it's good seeing the three of you together again."

Susan awkwardly appeared from behind the red shadows to join the three at the bar. Before anyone could respond, she continued.

"Oh, is that Foxy?"

Neshama nodded casually.

"I love that stuff!" Susan exclaimed.

Very unsurprising.

A shy smile appeared on Neshama's lips and she gently gestured to Susan to take a seat while preparing her turn. Her silver ring reflected the red light brightly.

Married.

"Sorry, I'm late. The protests are blocking public transport like crazy right now. No respect for the lockdown at all. Paradise is going cray cray."

Susan gestured her hands around wildly and thanked Neshama with a nod for the Foxy, then took her seat opposite Marguerite. Some of the pink powder had found its way into her red hair, making her look like a colourblind clown at a children's birthday party.

"The usual?" Neshama asked.

Helmut nodded while trying not to stare at Marguerite's hide, which sparkled extraordinarily and seemed to absorb the bar's light bizarrely.

Since the Fallen Bull incident, Susan and Helmut had made it their tradition to meet in the bar and discuss the case details over beers and cocktails, cigarettes and music, almost always accompanied by either Neshama or Marguerite and sometimes both. Of course, they didn't share any sensitive information, at least at first, but by now Neshama and Marguerite must have had a pretty good grasp of what was happening. For some odd reason, both Susan and Helmut seemed to trust the two.

"Thank you, Neshama."

High-pitched.

Susan handed a drink to Helmut.

"Cheers."

"Cheers. To the dead fox."

"To the fallen ape."

"To us."

"To us, indeed."

There was a short silence, at least as silent as it could

be with the heavy bass vibrations around them. The four quietly stared at their drinks. Though their laughter was relaxed and cheerful, all of them knew that this second death spelt more trouble than the first, not to mention the unrevealed slaughter of the ape.

A dark cloud had appeared over Paradise.

Neshama bit her lip and turned to Susan.

"Another one?"

"Well, I was gonna get drunk either way."

"Me too," Helmut grinned.

"Must have been a heavy couple of days, aye?"

Marguerite's soft voice was the only sound to ever have penetrated Helmut's systems and his quiet island was flooded in an instant.

"You have no idea."

"Still dreaming badly?"

Helmut nodded quietly and downed his drink.

Marguerite's hoof touched his hybrid skin and he met her green eyes once again. He knew she wanted to know more, but wouldn't ask while the other two were around.

Later.

"So, what's the reason for this festive gathering?", Neshama asked before taking another line.

"We have some stuff to discuss, as always."

Understanding showed on Neshama's face.

"I'll be over there if you need anything."

She got up and walked to the other side of the bar.

Marguerite followed her after a second, gently running her hoof through Helmut's hair.
Susan took a sip from her fiercely green cocktail and ran a hand through her own fiery hair, mimicking Marguerite's gesture.

Helmut laughed.

"Stop it. I know it's stupid."

"It's not stupid. It's cute."

"You're cute."

"No, I'm not."

"You really aren't," Helmut laughed.

Susan followed suit and her bright laugh seemed to build a wall from the loud bass music, which almost appeared to shout from the other side of the room.

"Should we open it?"

Helmut carefully laid the Ambassador's dark envelope on the bar.

"It's our only lead at this point, I guess."

"The only one worth pursuing anyway."

Without another word, Helmut tore the envelope open and emptied it. It contained a single piece of paper.

Energy levels spiking. Danger of overpowering systems.

"It's a bloody drawing of a bloody Centaur."

Infuriated. Calm systems.

Susan grabbed the paper and stared at it for a second.

"Oh that bloody cunt. Didn't she say this was gonna

be useful?"

"She also said the people we were looking for are called the Centaur. Which doesn't bloody help much." Helmut downed his drink furiously. He gestured Neshama over who already carried two new glasses, containing a notoriously black liquid. It reminded him of the dead fox's hide. Susan's voice broke his gaze.

"Wow. Helmut. You're never this… emotional."

Her words hung in the air for a few seconds almost as if they hadn't quite reached Helmut who seemed to stare into a distant void. Then he shook his head.

"I'm sorry. I'm just… a bit edgy, I guess. I was actually really calm before. I had no idea I was this charged."

Susan nodded understandingly.

"So, to recap, someone called the Centaur first killed the bull, then the fox who had just moments before stolen something the Ambassador needs back but cannot admit she even possessed. The Centaur must have known the fox, opening all sorts of possibilities, and the Ambassador knows it's the Centaur who is responsible for this because her operatives clashed with the Centaur's, for the lack of a more precise terminology, organisation. So, we can assume that her interests stand in stark contrast to theirs, given that she was telling the truth but I didn't detect any lies. Not more than usual anyhow. We don't know why they killed the bull, don't know what the fox stole or why he was killed for it and all we do know is that we need to find the Centaur and all the Ambassador has given us is a drawing of a creature which cannot physically exist."

"Seems like we're stuck in the same loop as always. Only this time, we're under lockdown, have a foreign power meddle in our investigation, and a bloody dead fox on our hands which will no doubt infuriate Fox Nation."

Helmut took a sip from his notoriously black drink.

Sweet. Surprising. Recalculating.

"Hm, yeah, the Councillor won't be amused."

"Neither am I right now."

Helmut grumpily grabbed the paper to tear it apart, but before he could, his eyes widened when he recognised the drawing for what it really was.

Recalculating. Recalculating. Recalculating.

"What? What is it, Helmut?"

Helmut didn't respond, the drawing entirely capturing his attention. Susan downed her drink and patiently waited. Seconds passed by, then minutes, and just then Marguerite walked by Helmut. But even her presence didn't make him look up. He remained utterly still, utterly focused, utterly breathless. For a moment, it seemed as if he would never take another breath. All the chaos around him, all the sounds, all the vibrations seemed to avoid him, running across the room, bouncing off walls and chairs, attempting everything not to reach Helmut whose body seemed to absorb everything. He had now closed his eyes and yet still seemed to stare into a distant void. Susan followed his process closely until her eyes sparked in surprise and recognition.

Then, in a sudden motion, his entire body shook, then shivered. Finally, his back straightened, he stretched his shoulders and when he opened his eyes, they were cold and dark and green. He took a single, sharp breath.

"I've seen this reaction before," Susan whispered, surprised.

"I've felt this before," Helmut responded equally quietly.

"The carvings. You had the same reaction when you first saw the carvings… only less intense, less consuming. Like, you almost didn't react to them at all, but you did go through the same procedure."

Helmut nodded.

"I didn't know you noticed. I barely noticed myself."

Susan gently laid her hand on his shoulder.

"You'd be surprised how much I see."

"Well then. The Ambassador has given us the second set of carvings, it appears."

"What do they mean? Why do you react to them like that?"

"I can't tell you, Susan. That is to say, I don't know."

He shook his head in disbelief.

"It just feels so real. Like, I know I've seen them before. They remind me of something. Both of them. I just don't know what it is, what it means. Not yet."

"How did the Ambassador get hold of the carvings of the Fallen Bull? And why would she give them to you?"

"No, Susan. It's not the same carvings. I'm not doing a great job explaining this."

Helmut took a deep breath.

"They're not the same carvings. It's a new set. And somehow, they're speaking to me. It's almost like they're telling me a story and I'm too stupid to listen."

Chapter Three

The Legend

Hours had passed since Helmut's revelations. The music had changed into a soft Indy soundtrack, the red light had dimmed down to just a shadow of its former self, and the crowd had grown and then returned to its original size, almost mirroring the tide at a beach, having left behind a somewhat wetter ground than before. Yet, Helmut and Susan were no closer to finding a solution to the little riddle the Ambassador seemed to be involved in. Having finished their respective shifts, both Neshama and Marguerite had joined the two at their table.

"There's something I have to tell you, Susan."

"What is it, Helmut?"

"The Ambassador. When she mentioned the Centaur. It wasn't the first time I heard that name."

"It wasn't?"

Helmut shook his head which lay on Marguerite's shoulder.

"The very first time the word appeared in my mind was right when you walked through the projection of the Fallen Bull and its carvings. Then, later, in one of my dreams, my friend appeared and mentioned the Centaur. He said I was supposed to find the Centaur. Until now, I thought that was just a mere coincidence. Like my subconscious simply created that dream because, well, you looked like a centaur for a second. It's not until now that I believe there's a deeper meaning to it."

Susan starred at Helmut. Then she laughed.

"That's all? Find the Centaur? Well, it seems like that's exactly what we're supposed to do. Your subconscious seems to be a much better detective than you ever could be, Helmut."

Somewhat relieved Helmut grinned, well-knowing that he hadn't told the entire story just yet.

"There's more to this than meets the eye," Marguerite carefully whispered almost as if she was uncertain whether she should speak up or not.

All eyes turned to her, and for a second, it seemed like she regretted speaking up, though, of course, it had been nothing more than a quiet whisper.

Helmut gently squeezed her leg.

"Do tell."

"It's not the first time I hear the name the Centaur either. Not that I thought it mattered much earlier. There's a story unknown to most. Right before the Oracle died, she is said to have had another vision. It's an old fairytale in cow legend for the Oracle was the first attempt to create my race."

"The same Oracle which foretold the 'He who is promised' prophecy?"

"The one and only," Neshama laughed.

Susan rolled her eyes almost as if she wanted to dismiss the idea. The Oracle was a myth herself that nobody quite believed in anymore these days.

"What vision?" Helmut asked because he wanted to listen to Marguerite's voice more than anything else.

"She foresaw the Centaur."

Helmut and Susan stared at her.

"She foresaw the Centaur? What do you mean?"

"You're kidding me, right? She's nothing more than a myth."

Marguerite smiled.

"She's no more a myth than your impossible Centaur is."

Helmut shrugged.

"I love a bit of a mystery."

"I am fond of a good story," Susan agreed expectantly.

Neshama chuckled and filled their glasses. Then, Marguerite began to speak and her voice captured Helmut in an instant.

"It was a time of suffering and despair for the Alliance. The Kaiserpaar had reigned for decades, but even they couldn't stop the beginnings of the Last War. In a desperate attempt to survive, the Alliance created fighting AI like the world had never seen before. Under the guidance of General Sig, the borders were slowly

stabilised. Meanwhile, across the channel, the Alliance's scientists proceeded to clone animals. Though many of the attempts had been successful, none of the creatures survived for longer than a few hours. Many had died and even more would die. Until one day, the unthinkable happened. Through a mere accident, the genes of a cow and a human were paired together, creating the first surviving clone; the Oracle. When she opened her eyes, they were sharp and bright and lively, and the scientists knew that they had succeeded where all the others had failed. But then, the cow spoke, and her voice was dark and full of despair, so terrible that it is said to have shattered glass and broken walls. She spoke the words of the Prophecy as we all know it today. Then, her body collapsed, blood pouring out of her eyes and ears and mouth. She was thought dead and an unspeakable silence overcame everyone who had witnessed this miracle. But when the scientists came to study her body, the dead creature spoke once more. She spoke of a beautiful future, full of happiness and delight, of bright stars and even brighter creatures. She spoke of those who would come together to form Paradise, and she spoke of those who'd live under its rule, in peace and quiet. She spoke of those who'd die to create Paradise and she spoke of those who would suffer because of it. And then, she spoke of the Centaur. Her voice was sharp like a sword and the scientists' ears began to bleed. Her eyes were glowing like the stars and the scientists' eyes were blinded. Her words were harsh like the Northern wind and they tore the scientists' souls apart. Her words were like nothing they had ever heard. Nor would they ever hear anything like her wisdom again for she spoke the truth that day. And no other truth has been spoken since then.

When those who seek to harm Paradise
Are heralded by the Centaur
When those who seek to save Paradise
Are heralded by him who is promised

Turn East for you will find salvation
Where nobody dares to look
Turn West for you will find resolve
Where nobody dares to search

Turn North for you will find friends
Where nobody expects to gain
Turn South for you will need to escape
Where nobody expects you to flee

Then, her body collapsed once more, surrounded by crying, bleeding, shattered scientists. And thus, my people were born.

Marguerite's voice ended the story as softly as she had begun, tears running down her cheeks. They dropped onto the wooden table with a familiar sound. Popp. Popp. Popp. Helmut felt like he was seeing Marguerite for the first time. Really seeing her, not just looking at her. He understood now that she honestly did believe in the Prophecy, and that she truly did believe this legend. He absorbed everything about her. The wet eyes which showed no sign of drying up, the short hide still sparkling despite the story, the muscles underneath her skin and the gentle look she gave him. She truly did believe it, and for a second, just the fraction of a second, Helmut understood why. But then, Susan's bright laugh ripped his understanding apart.

"So, basically, you're saying that the Centaur is like the four apocalyptic horsemen?"

"No, the Centaur is the saviour."

"What now?"

"He's said to free those who aren't free."

Certainty.

Helmut tilted his head slightly so he could watch Marguerite's face. The tears had slowly dried up, but the conviction hadn't left her eyes.

"I don't get it."

"The cow scholars studying the legend of the Centaur believe that when the Centaur rises, all those who were suppressed will be freed."

“But isn’t the Centaur in the Greek legends a mix of human and horse? Where’s the cow coming in?”

“Horse, donkey, cow… we all have four legs and a booty for the Gods. Who says that in this day and age, a centaur can’t be a mix of human and cow genes? My ancestors used to be exactly that.”

“Who says it needs to be a cow anyway?” Helmut inserted himself into the heated exchange.

“Well, it’s a cow fairytale. I’d assume the protagonist is at least somewhat… well, cow-ish.”

Neshama laughed brightly, and the tension that had gripped the table left as quickly as it had arrived.

“Just one last question,” Helmut added. “The Centaur. The myth. The legend. Is the Centaur in these stories metaphorical or do you believe that it, indeed, comes in the shape of an actual centaur, whether it’s a horse or a cow doesn’t really matter at this point.”

Marguerite sighed.

“I don’t know. I want to believe it’s an actual centaur, like in the stories, but that’d be impossible. Our scientists have run too many experiments over the past decades. It’s impossible. So it must be metaphorical.”

“So, then the Centaur, could they be anyone?”, Susan asked, her voice oddly interested after she had dismissed the entire idea before.

Marguerite nodded.

“I guess so, yeah. It’s a legend. I believe that when the

Centaur appears, they free those who are suppressed."

Susan looked thoughtful for a second.

"Out with it, Susan. I know that look."

"Well, bear with me for a second. But if the Centaur is a legend, and a metaphorical one at that, and then the Ambassador gives us the drawing of a creature which doesn't actually exist, which is the second carving, directly related to the murders. Then these carvings must mean something different than we anticipated."

"You mean it's not a message to Councillor Christine after all?"

"I don't know. It might still be. Or it might be something different entirely. The only thing I know is that we find ourselves in a game much larger than us and I can't shake the feeling that we're nothing more than pawns at this stage."

Helmut grinned wickedly.

"Why are you smiling like that, Helmut?"

"Because sometimes, the pawns become the most valuable pieces on the board."

He raised his glass.

"To the pawns."

"To us," the others returned.

Chapter Four

Mathena

"Hell rained down from the sky that day. We were pinned down by mortar fire and the Donian troops closed in on our position. We returned fire, but our defences were quickly overrun. I watched my friends die one by one."

Jack was sitting in a chair. His shoulders were straight as a blade, his naked body sharp and toned, and his hands handcuffed behind his back. For the agents around him, he looked as calm as one could be when being interrogated in a black site. But inside him, the hell of that day seethed.

"Please continue, Mr Millar," Dumbo requested.

"Of course."

Jack didn't actually know his name or any of his interrogators' names for that matter, so he had given them nicknames based on their appearance.

"As I said, we were pinned down. There was no escaping the inevitable. I watched as my fellow soldiers, my friends, died one by one. Taking bullets to the head, to the chest. Ricky took five to the chest and still managed to take a few of the bastards down."

Jack paused and looked around the all-too-familiar

room. There was nothing here that would give away his location. Only black walls and men in black clothes.

“We retreated to our last haven, the basement. We held them off long enough to gain a way into the canalisation. My Commanding Officer chose me to get our intel back to our base. You must understand, I didn’t want to leave. I begged her to send somebody else, but she insisted it was me.”

Jack took a deep breath and tried to hold the tears back. It wasn’t right to cry here. He was a hardened Californian soldier, not a little Donian crybaby.

“It was the hardest thing I have ever done. Leaving my friends behind to be killed by you bastards. Not a day goes by that I don’t think about them. Ricky. Mason. Hanna. Conny. Every goddamn day I see their faces in the mirror. Every goddamn day I wish it was me who had stayed behind to cover one of them instead of going myself.”

“That’s all very poetic, Mr Millar, but none of this touches upon why we are here today. You promised us information on the Californian troop movements and the intel you were tasked to protect that day.”

So they still hadn’t managed to crack the code. Jack didn’t doubt for a second that they would have disposed of his body immediately if they didn’t require him for that.

“I’m getting there.”

Nine-Fingers looked like he'd hit him again, but refrained.

Of course, none of them knew that he had absolutely no idea how to decrypt the intel.

"Hurry up. It's my wife's birthday and I'd hate to miss it."

"Come on, buddy, we both know that nobody would freely wed you. Even if you had all ten fingers left."

Jack cursed his quick tongue already before he felt the pain in his groin. He had been stalling them for days and he rapidly ran out of believable lies to tell them. His last resort then.

"Damn, yeah. That's the good stuff."

Nine-Fingers hit him again and darkness welcomed Jack in its endless embrace.

When he woke again, the room was empty.

"Damn, those people are dumb," he muttered through the pain.

"They are, aren't they?"

Jack jumped upright into the air, leaving the chair behind him. Confused, he stared at his untied hands.

"Damn it. Who the fuck are you?"

A woman in a tight black suit stood in front of him.

"I don't think you're in a position to ask any questions, Jack."

"Fuck you, then. Go on and torture me like the rest of

the idiots here. I'm a god damn loyal soldier, not a traitor. I don't the fuck know what else I'm supposed to tell you. Just get it done."

"Relax, buddy. I'm with the Agency."

"Oh, right, and the others aren't? Get your stories straight."

The stranger exhaled visibly.

"I'm with the CIA."

"I know that you're with the Central Intelligence Agency."

The stranger laughed. It resounded loudly from the tight walls around them.

"Not quite. I'm with the other one."

Jack's eyes narrowed.

"You're Californian."

"They told me you'd be quick."

"Fuck you, motherfucker. I don't believe a single word coming out of your Donian mouth. Make fun of me one more time, I dare you."

The woman chuckled.

"I'd love to see you trying to take me down. I really do. Come on, buddy. Gimme your best."

Jack found himself lying on the floor quicker than a New York bagel.

"Now, will you sit down and listen to me? I don't want to hurt you, but I will if you insist."

Jack's eyes wandered through the room. There was

nobody here but the new stranger. He'd take his chances against a single enemy any time of the day.

"Don't, buddy. Don't do it."

Jack readied his body and prepared to charge when the stranger held up a hand.

"Sit down, and I'll let you in on a little secret. What do you think will happen even if you'd take me down? Those doors are heavily sealed. You wouldn't even make it out of this room."

"I'd take you hostage and make them open it for me."

"And what makes you think I'm worth anything at all, or even more than the first Californian spec-ops soldier we've had the pleasure of interrogating?"

For the first time in a long while, Jack smiled an honest smile. He knew when he was being tested. Whatever this was, it was more than an interrogation. This just became a negotiation, though he didn't quite understand why yet.

"Well, there's the fact that you're in this room alone with me. Nobody has been alone with me so far. Either you're competent, or powerful. Probably both. Since you've entered, all cameras have shut off, so either you're here to kill me or to offer me something off the record. And while your appearance makes you look just like any other regular suit, I recognise a battle-scarred soldier when I see one. You're just like me if I'm not mistaken. Should you be here to kill me, just do it now.

I'm done with this war."

"How's that?"

"Haven't you listened? I have watched my friends die, have been captured by the enemy and after all I've done for California, nobody has come to my rescue. Every day I see the dead faces of my friends. The dead, empty eyes where a soul was once speaking to me. Every day. They never leave me. I don't want anyone else to die in this war. But that can't be. So take me out now. Set me free."

"I really gotta talk to my colleagues outside. How the hell didn't they manage to get a single word out of you when all it takes is to listen to you for a second."

Jack looked up from his hands, not holding his tears back anymore.

"You tricked me," he exhaled.

"You must forgive them. They're rookies. It's their first time interrogating someone on their own actually."

Jack laughed a helpless laugh.

"I will die before I forgive any of these Clone monks."

"And you're sure you don't just want to tell us about the intel?"

He sighed.

"Well, I guess, if you ask this nicely I don't have any other choice, do I?"

"You know, Jo, for a dead man, there's plenty of life left in you."

Jack's eyes widened and for a second, he lost control

over his facial expression.

The woman laughed brightly.

"Damn, soldier, you just looked as if you've seen the Easter bunny penetrating Santa unprotected."

"How do you know that name?"

"I told you, I'm with the CIA."

"You're no more Californian than my grandma is German."

"Fuck's sake, soldier. They warned me you're untrusting, but I had no idea."

"Who's they?"

"Now, here are your options. A: I'll give you the bullet you've been begging for ever since you've been captured. B: I leave and you stay here and eventually die of boredom. Or C: you follow my lead and we're getting the fuck out of here."

"Right, because you're just gonna let me walk out of here freely."

The woman chuckled and opened the door to the corridor. Two bodies lay in a pool of wet blood. Jack moved closer to the door to get a better look. Dumbo and Nine-Fingers.

"Where's Pity-Face?"

"Who now?"

"Guy with a face so ugly, I pitied him for it despite being a Donian. Nobody deserves to be that ugly."

"Ah, he's in the control room. Together with a few

others. I gotta say, security was tight here."

She held the door open for Jack. He hesitantly walked towards it, expecting a trap any second. His eyes continued to scan his surroundings carefully.

"Okay then, let's go."

He stepped out of the room he had been held captive in for so long. He quickly checked for weapons on the dead bodies, but his saviour seemed to have disposed of them.

"It seems I owe you."

"Oh, Jack, you do. So badly."

"And who might I owe this badly?"

The woman smiled with her eyes, her face entirely expressionless.

"You may call me Mathena."

Chapter Five

First Contact

The sun stands brightly on the horizon. I check my rifle's safety catch before I look up to Syphilis. He grins at me.

"Time to move."

I nod and line up behind a few of my compatriots. Syphilis is right behind me, laying his hand reassuringly on my shoulder. His tight grip calms me down.

"First time across the Canal. Are you ready?"

I nod again and give him a weak smile. This isn't what I had expected when I woke up this morning, but it is what it is. I don't question my orders. I fulfil them, no questions asked.

"You all packed?"

Syphilis smiles a beautiful smile, almost as bright as the sun.

"Ready for duty."

I chuckle at our inside joke. Then I start moving, slowly at first, then faster when my mates increase their pace. Thirty-one bodies jogging in sync. For a moment I wish I could watch us in action before I realise that I am part of it. That's what I have trained for all my life. Finally, the day has come.

Our squad moves onto the ferry and a few seconds

later, we are crossing the Canal. Nobody knows what is awaiting us on the other side. I look around, can feel the cold water on my face, know that the wind is playing with my hair. I check my magazine. Ready for duty.

We spread out and slowly walk through the forest. The thick leaves provide us with welcome cover from the hot sunbeams. It feels more humid than it ever has in Paradise. We stride through the shadows, our weapons always handy. Though we have sent out scouts, there is a certain level of unease among the squad. This is unknown territory. Our satellites and Eagle scouts couldn't look through the forest cover. It would be too easy to prepare an ambush here. We are almost inviting them to do just that. Even more so, since this is the first time in decades that Paradise is sending infantry across the Canal. There's no way of knowing what is out here, or if there is anything out here at all. The refugee influx from the Last War had stopped a long time ago. We don't know the terrain, don't know what is around the next corner, don't know the vegetation. All of this and more, we are sent to investigate.

"It's almost like in the old movies, isn't it?" Syphilis quietly whispers into my ear.

"Which ones?"

I'm no big fan of any movies, let alone pre-Paradise ones.

"The old ones. Almost ancient by now. The few who survived the Last War. Those telling the tales of heroic soldiers fighting for kingdom and glory."

"You mean stupidity and patriotism?", I laugh.

"Indeed," Syphilis grins.

He loves those movies. They are his guilty pleasure, though those movies are banned by order of the First Councillor. A lot of pre-Paradise things are forbidden these days.

"I recently watched one which took place in ancient Greece. A real nailbiter."

Syphilis looks down at his hands only to find them wearing combat gloves.

"Oh please, not again."

"It was brutal. It was brilliant. It was utterly breathtaking."

"No matter what I do, you're going to tell me anyhow, aren't you?"

"I sure am," he grins.

"So, then, make it short and sweet."

"Story of your love life, isn't it?"

I roll my eyes, though he has a point.

"Fine. Tell me the glorious tale."

"You would have liked it. It has your favourite actor in it. Gerard something..."

"The good-looking guy with that three-day beard who always looks like he just can't be arsed but always is?",

I ask more excitedly than I would like to admit.

"Yes. He's the bad guy. Some Greek god. He and his sister are awfully close. Too close, if you know what I mean. She's a god, obviously, but looks more like an animal than human, really. Then again, who knows how gods looked like back then anyway. Or today, for that matter."

A silent smile appears on my lips. Encouraged, Syphilis continues.

"They live a happy, exciting life. Here and there, they're bothered by humanity, but in the greater scheme of things, they can do whatever they want to. Until one day, they discover that the Titans, their ancient antagonists, aren't dead at all, merely caged underneath the oldest of the old volcanoes. Everything the gods ever thought to be true about their world collapses and they're faced with a dilemma."

"Let me guess," I interrupt him. "They disagree over what to do and thus, the tragic tale continues."

Syphilis gives me a sour look, but I know he isn't furious.

"Just, you know, let me tell the story please."

"Fine, you may continue," I laugh at the childish expression on his face.

"So, they discover the Titans in a place where they shouldn't be. They shouldn't even exist. For all the two Gods know, it should be impossible for them to exist.

They were destroyed by the eldest of all Gods a long time ago. A long, long time ago. So long ago, it even seems ancient to the gods themselves. That sorta timespan we're talking about here. But they exist, inexplicably. Suddenly, everything the two know and hold dear seems under threat. What to do? What to do?"

"But," I interrupt him again.

"Yes?"

"The Titans are locked up under that volcano, aren't they? How are they supposed to threaten the almighty gods themselves?"

"Just, you know. They pose a threat. Don't always question everything. It's a really annoying habit you developed while you were on mission."

I grin.

"So, the two gods have to decide what they want to do about it. But they disagree. The Gerard God wants to speak to the Titans and make their existence known to all other gods whereas the other one wants to kill the Titans, who cannot be killed, once and for all."

"But...?"

Now Syphilis rolls his eyes.

"If they cannot be killed, how does the other god want to kill them?"

"She's a god, she'll manage."

"But all other gods have failed before her."

"Well, maybe she's special. Just, let me tell the story,

okay? It's a good one."

"Fine."

I grab my weapon tighter. I would never understand why Syphilis loves those movies that much. They are stupid.

"So, she tells the Gerard god that she's d'accord with his plan to make the Titans' existence known, but behind his back, she plots against him and when the time comes, she literally stabs him in the back. He bleeds out in front of her, all hope shattered, his eyes sad and shocked by her betrayal. She goes on to free the Titans' and let them destroy humanity which she always hated."

"That's dark."

"The old Greeks had a thing for the dramatic, I reckon."

Before we can continue our banter, out of nowhere, there's a sound like a squashed melon. Before I know what is happening, my mate's head explodes right in front of me and I'm blinded by blood and brain.

Shots fired. Silencers used. Ambush.

Blindly, I throw myself onto the ground, praying to the ancient Greek gods that I have cover. I know there's nothing I can do for my mate, but I drag him with me behind a few rocks. His body feels heavy, though his blood is leaking all over the place. I loosen my grip and his body falls to the ground and lays there silently. I don't even know which one he is. His entire face is gone.

"We're under heavy fire. Request immediate air support."

I realise my internal comms are still functioning.

"This is R941120. One down. Unknown tangos. Requesting immediate update."

I calmly transmit my position via our internal comms system. Quickly, the others are calling in their situations. I see flashes of their situations in front of me. My systems visualise the contested area in a 4D-model.

Five down. Fire from three directions. Unknown tangos.

I search the visualisation, hoping to find Syphilis.

"This is HQ. Air support is 30 minutes out. You're on your own until then. Good luck."

"Damn it," a voice next to me yells.

Startled by the physical voice, I turn around to Syphilis, who gives me a cheeky smile.

"Let's go, Helmut. That's what we've been training for all our lives. Let's give those barbarians a taste of our steel."

Syphilis always prefers to actually talk instead of using the silent internal comms system.

Despite everything, a sinister smile reaches my lips.

"On three," I hear myself say.

"One."

I turn off my weapon's safety catch.

"Two."

I take a deep, relaxing breath.

"Three."

I look into Syphilis's eyes. They're dark and sharp and utterly happy and for a moment, just the fraction of a second, he looks like an ancient god.

Chapter Six

The Test

"Ah, there you are."

"Here we are."

Helmut tilted his head and looked at the stranger in front of him.

"What is this about?" Susan asked casually.

They hadn't even reached their office in the Police Headquarters. It seemed to be a busy morning. Ever since the lockdown, the police needed to be a lot more alert than before. Helmut watched as a squad of third-gen police robots jogged to their recharge station.

"It's pee-in-a-cup time."

"It's what now?" both of them exclaimed.

"It's a regularly mandated drug test."

Helmut and Susan shared a knowing look.

Danger.

It wasn't the good news they were hoping for.

"I haven't even had my first cup of coffee."

"You can have one after the test."

"Today is not a good day for that. We have a meeting with the Fox Ambassador tomorrow which we have to prepare for. We'll do it another time."

"I'm afraid I must insist," the tiny gelding said.

Reasoning failed. Recalculating.

"Before we go any further I usually like to know who I'm talking to," Helmut interjected politely.

"I'm Special Agent Ian."

"Nice to meet you, Special Agent Ian. My name is…"

"I'm aware of who you are. I'm here to drug-test you, not let you sweet-talk me. They warned me about you."

"They?"

"My superiors. If you'd please follow me. I don't have all day."

The gelding's right hoof made an inarticulate gesture.

Last resort then. Threatening behaviour activated.

"And I'm afraid we don't answer to the Department's policies. We exist outside your structure. Please take up any formal complaints with our secretary. You'll find him right in our offices."

"I'm afraid you don't exist outside our hierarchy," the gelding insisted.

His huge eyes looked awfully misplaced next to his wide teeth which grinned arrogantly.

"Well, let me contact Councillor Christine then," Susan said.

"I'm sure she'll be delighted to fire your arse for blocking an important investigation."

"Please do. But I could also just tell you that the orders to test you came directly from her Office."

Helmut and Susan froze in stunned silence. Three

bulls walked by idly chatting about the latest movie.

Unexpected. Recalculating.

Two tall geldings appeared behind Susan and Helmut, wearing long white coats.

Internal Affairs.

"Let's not make a big deal out of this. Either you'll submit to the drug test, or I have you escorted out of the building in front of everyone."

"Fine," Susan grunted.

Surprising.

They began to move towards the toilets, the gelding rather excitedly, Helmut and Susan rather not.

"What are you doing?" Helmut whispered underneath his breath.

"Taking the goddamn drug test."

"You're gonna fail that stupid thing."

Susan shrugged her shoulders carelessly.

"We'll see about that."

Helmut raised an eyebrow and ran his hand through his hair. A few streaks floated to the ground. He recognised the familiar rhythm of the geldings' four-hooved walk behind him. What was usually a comforting and relaxing sound now felt like a ticking bomb.

"How can you be so calm?"

"It wouldn't do me much good if I freaked out right in front of them, would it?"

"No," Helmut admitted, still surprised by her calm demeanour.

"That would probably give away how shit scared I am right now. I knew I'd fool them, but I didn't know you were this easily played as well. Maybe I shouldn't trust your observing skills, after all."

Helmut pursed his lips, then exhaled slightly and squeezed Susan's hand. It was an unfamiliar gesture for him, but one which, he hoped, would provide her with comfort.

"Listen. Worst case, the test will be positive. We'll appeal the results. That'll take a while and we can still get on with our investigation. Until then, stay calm, okay. We got this."

Suspicious. Alert.

"Ah, here we are," the gelding proclaimed.

Slimy tone.

The gelding pushed the door to the washrooms open with its big head.

"You first," he pointed to Susan.

The wait was killing Helmut. His systems ran fast and hot, energy rays spiking through his hybrid body every other second. He tried not to show any of it, but he caught himself pacing through the tiny room in which he waited for Susan and the gelding to be back. The gelding's colleagues stood outside the door and he couldn't help but feel like a prisoner.

Applying cooling procedure. Immediate impact.

Helmut took a deep breath and felt his body relax a bit. Sweat poured from his hybrid skin. He ran his hand through his hair. Finally, he recognised Susan's voice when she entered the room.

"Let's see what the two of you have been up to then," Ian grinned.

Attempted devilish grin. Failure.

Ian put their urine samples into a small white device.

Fifth-generation drug tester. Rapid test system. Immediate analysis.

"How the fuck does that idiot have any sway over our future?", he whispered to Susan.

Despite the severity of their situation, or maybe because of it, she laughed a bright laugh. Ian turned around to the two and stared at them for a long second. Then, his device beeped, and he smugly turned around to welcome the results.

"No, that's impossible."

"What, exactly, is impossible?" Susan asked smugly.

"Your tests. They're… no, that's impossible."

"Excuse me, Special Agent Ian, would you please answer my colleague's question?"

The gelding turned around, his eyes wide in anger.

Increased whiteness.

"I'm afraid you're free to go. Your tests were

negative. Of course, that's only the preliminary results."

"Of course," Susan nodded. "I'm glad the system still works. These checks and balances are critical to keeping the system honest. Keep up the good work, Special Agent Ian."

"How dare you speak to me in that tone?", the skinny gelding exploded fumingly.

Helmut stepped forward.

"I'd be cautious, Ian. One more word and I'll have you escorted out of the building. For your own protection, of course. I wouldn't want our drug-free Susan here to accidentally hurt your arrogant little tongue. In fact, why don't I step back and let the two of you sort this out."

As promised, Helmut stepped back, exposing the gelding's skinny body to a wickedly smiling Susan.

"Come now, Helmut. Let that poor soul be. He's been devastated by the results already, no need for physical retribution."

She paused slightly as if she was thinking.

"Unless, of course, he doesn't get out of my face immediately."

He did.

A short while later, Helmut and Susan walked through the headquarters' extensive corridors towards their office. A slightly confused smile covered Helmut's face.

"So, how did you do it?"

"A lady has many secrets."

"You're no lady."

"How dare you, Helmut? I'm the most ladiest lady of all of them."

Deflecting. Recurring pattern.

"Well, I was about to apologise for taking away your agency earlier and defending you, but since you're a lady, that seems rather appropriate. I wouldn't have wanted you to get your precious ladyfingers dirty."

Susan giggled lightly.

"You have a comeback for everything, don't you?"

"It's my job, I'm afraid."

"And here I thought your job was catching a freely roaming killer in Paradise which we have absolutely no clue on how to find."

"Way to ruin our victory over the system, Susan."

But despite their situation, his eyes smiled. They hadn't enjoyed many victories lately, and he'd take anything at this point, even if it was one over a miserable gelding.

"That wasn't a victory. That was survival."

"Sometimes, victory and survival mean the same thing."

"But not always."

"Nothing always means the same."

"In that case, there's one thing left for us to find out

though. Amongst the whole "who killed the bull and fox" thingy."

"Amongst that, of course."

Helmut stopped by one of the enormous windows. Snowflakes endlessly attacked the glass like a bulletstorm. Susan tilted her head slightly. For now, the attack seemed unable to penetrate the building.

"Why the fuck did Councillor Christine mandate us to take that drug test?"

"And why now?" Susan added.

"The way I see it, there are three possibilities here. One, it was random."

"I think we can pretty much exclude that."

"Agreed. Two: She expected the tests to be positive and hold it over our heads for leverage."

"Possibly, but we haven't given her any reason to doubt us yet. Nor will we."

"You mean, outside of our lack of any substantial progress and internally declaring her a person of interest in the investigation at some point."

Helmut laughed.

"Well, yeah. But she couldn't possibly know about that."

"That only leaves option three. She wanted to get rid of us."

Or one of us.

Helmut was painfully aware that the Councillor didn't

attempt to get him excluded from the investigation. She knew he was a robot. She knew that even if he had taken drugs, it would never show in the reports. His system's filters cleared every toxic substance immediately. So, this had been a targeted attack on Susan. Only, he couldn't tell her that without giving away his true identity. That would never be an option. His instructions permitted it.

"That does seem like the most logical explanation."

"But why?"

"Either for our lack of results, but given the secrecy of this operation, I doubt she'd want to include more people. So, maybe we're closer to a breakthrough than we think."

"A breakthrough that involves her?"

"Maybe. It's pure speculation at this point. But we have to tread lightly."

"Agreed."

"Alright, that's enough speculation for now. We have a trap to prepare."

Susan turned around and walked towards her office, leaving a thoughtful Helmut behind. He watched the never-ending snowflakes arriving in Paradise, their movement a complex and unpredictable puzzle even to his sharp mind. He almost seemed to have fallen asleep when his eyes widened. A sad smile immediately covered his lips and he sighed deeply when he realised what the recent events truly meant.

Re-assessing assets. Recalculating.

Chapter Seven

The Fox Ambassador

Helmut opened his eyes. It was snowing.

Unsurprising.

It hadn't really stopped snowing since it had started a few weeks ago and at first, the snow had melted as quickly as it had fallen. But then, little by little, more snow fell than could melt and, over time, the snow covered the City and much of Paradise. It was only early in the afternoon, but already the skies were beginning to darken, highlighting the colourful contrast even further.

"I love some more snow."

Susan's cheerful voice interrupted his train of thought.

"What is it with you and your constant happiness about everything?"

"Ever heard of cheerful nihilism?"

Helmut rolled his eyes.

"You can't be cheerful and a nihilist."

"Watch me," Susan giggled.

"Susan?"

"Yes, my dear?"

"What's that pink powder coming out of your vast nostrils?"

Her left hand self-consciously went up to her human

nose to find nothing of the sort.

"Oh, you got me, Helmut. You got me good."

Helmut grinned before a serious expression covered his face.

"Did you take it for breakfast or lunch?"

Susan's cheerful expression faded and she remained quiet.

"Or both?"

"Neither."

Liar.

"If you say so, Susan. Just don't let it cloud your judgment. I'm relying on you. We came way too close to mayhem with that stupid drug test."

She looked like she wanted to wish him to hell but then decided not to.

Helmut grinned at her again.

"Now, are you ready to have some fun?"

"How much fun?"

"The most fun."

"Are you finally telling me where we're going?"

"I don't have to," he said and pointed to an expansive, glamorous building.

It stood tall against the incoming snow, almost becoming one with it. White on white. The crystals on the walls brightly reflected the last light of the day, blinding anyone looking too closely. Grim-looking foxes patrolled the walls, holding small but powerful guns in their hands. Drones flew high above the building, covering all angles. Fox Embassy.

"Excuse the wait, my dear friends. Important business and all that. I'm afraid I can't go into detail."

Sleek voice. Tiny fox. Psychological issues expected.

Helmut turned around to the fox. He wore a tight tuxedo. His vast tail swung behind him in the air, almost as if he tried to take up more space than his tiny body possibly could.

"Mr Ambassador, it's a great honour. Thank you for taking some time for us out of your busy schedule."

Susan bowed politely in front of the fox who barely reached her knees. Helmut followed suit, though his bow didn't go quite as deep as Susan's.

"Oh, no need for that," the Ambassador claimed though Helmut sensed the pleasure in his voice.

Issues confirmed.

Flatter. Wheedle. Blarney.

A smile that could have been mistaken for shyness ran across Susan's lips. Helmut barely managed to suppress his own.

"Honoured Mr Ambassador, we're hoping to steal some of your valued time in order to shed some light onto recent events in the City."

"Please, my friends, it'd be my honour. Take a seat, if you'd like."

With the agility unique to foxes, he jumped onto his own, elevated armchair. After Susan and Helmut sat down, he was almost on their height. Almost.

"How may I be of service to you?"

"We're here because of the dead fox in the City park."

"Yes, yes, a tragic incident, no doubt. Have you caught the killer yet?"

"Not yet, honoured Mr Ambassador, but we have our best team on it."

"I'm glad to hear that. It's indeed a travesty that it had to come to this. A killing, right here in Paradise. That must be a first."

Helmut tilted his head slightly in surprise. He felt Susan arriving at the same conclusion. Did he not know about the bull murder cover-up, or did he merely play a game?

Proceed with caution.

"Be that as it may, we have absolutely no idea who the fox may be. He's not registered in any of our systems and we couldn't find any sort of ID on him. We were hoping that you could shed some light on this."

The small fox nodded.

"I'd be glad to be of service to Paradise."

"We greatly appreciate your cooperation, Mr Ambassador."

Helmut looked through the Ambassador's office. It smelled oddly familiar here, though he didn't know why.

There was something about this building, and this room in particular, which felt awfully familiar. But he had never been here before. That, he was sure about.

"Did you bring a DNA sample?"

"We did, indeed," Susan replied and handed a small translucent bag to the fox.

He quickly grabbed it with his paws and emptied its contents onto a piece of machinery on his desk.

Standard DNA-reader. Third generation. Fox specified.

The reader scanned the DNA sample, then flashed a green light.

"Ah, you're in luck. His identity isn't classified by our Government."

"Lucky indeed."

The fox moved to the printer on the far side of the room and grabbed the printed analysis.

"It appears the dead fox is part of a visiting performing troupe in honour of Paradise's anniversary. His name is Kristian Dioti. He's well known among my fellow compatriots. I've seen him perform a couple of times. He was truly gifted, though not easy on the eye if you know what I mean."

The Ambassador handed the sheet over to Susan, plain sorrow in his voice.

Helmut tilted his head again.

No lies detected.

"Thank you, Mr Ambassador. This will be most helpful."

"Of course. I have one request to make, however. My Government would very much appreciate it if we could assist you in your investigation. No fox has ever been slain in Paradise. You'll understand that this has caused quite the stir on the island. We'd greatly appreciate it if we were to be involved in the investigation."

"Mr Ambassador, I'm afraid that's beyond my paygrade", Helmut said with just enough disappointment in his voice.

"You'll have to address Cow Councillor Christine on this matter. You diplomats will figure it out."

The fox nodded.

"I figured as much, but thank you regardless. Would you do me the honour of being my dinner guests sometime instead? I'm sure we have a lot to talk about over the next few weeks."

The words stood loudly in the room, the plain intent visible for everyone. Finally, just when the ensuing silence was about to become uncomfortable, Helmut nodded.

"It'd be my great honour to attend one of your dinner parties, Mr Ambassador."

"Indeed," Susan added. "Rumour has it, they're quite spectacular."

"I do fancy myself as quite the host," the fox blushed.

“We’re looking forward to your official invitation then, Mr Ambassador.”

“Thank you again, Mr Ambassador. You’ve been more than helpful. We deeply appreciate your cooperation.”

“Fox Nation stands at your service.”

When they finally left the Embassy, it was dark and cold. Snow still continued to fall, covering everything around the two. It would have been a winter wonderland if it wasn’t for the lockdown. Not a soul walked through the freshly fallen snow. Except for the patrolling robots.

So not a soul at all.

Susan walked Helmut home and though the streets were empty and vast, the City still whistled and sang its own little song. It was difficult to hear at first, but once the two started listening, they heard it. Listened to the million voices which lived in the City, sensed the presence of all the Great Nine creatures, felt the hope of those sleeping, and the unrest of those who were still awake. They could almost feel them all. All of them but one. They stood tall and dark on top of a mountain just at the edges of the City, a terrible smile covering their face.

Chapter Eight

The Date

Though he didn't feel the cold himself, Helmut sensed Marguerite's distinct displeasure. He sensed it like he hadn't sensed anything before. It was so clear, so crystal-clear right in front of him. Then, she smiled over his offer to hand her his coat and he tumbled and though he was trying to keep his balance, it didn't quite work. When he fell, he knew he should feel pain, but there was nothing but fire in his chest. Hot, fierce fire.

Trouble.

Marguerite laughed brightly and extended her hoof to help Helmut from the ground. He graciously accepted her help and got back to his feet. Snow dripped from his hair.

"Well, I don't think this one will do you any good now."

Helmut held his snow-covered coat into the air.

"Is it dry on the inside?", Marguerite laughed.

"It is," Helmut admitted, surprised, after he checked the inside.

"You may then."

"Yes, my lady," he grinned.

Gently, Helmut used the coat to cover her rear. He

couldn't quite resist taking a look at her pink udders. The teats stood out in the cold.

He felt an unfamiliar urge to suck on them.

How can something be so simple, yet so beautiful?

Before Marguerite could notice, he was back at her side.

"Ah, that feels good," she sighed contentedly.

"It's my distinct honour to serve you."

"Stop it. You ain't the Fox Ambassador."

Helmut laughed.

"Word got around then?"

"He's a well-known cock around my circles."

Helmut tilted his head slightly towards her.

"Care to share?"

Marguerite gently shook her head.

"Your rules, Helmut. No talk about work today."

"But I meant my work."

"It applies to all work, especially mine."

Gentle teasing. Firm. New topic.

"Fine," he rolled his eyes.

She laughed.

There was a short silence when both of them just walked side by side through the street. Helmut looked back the way they came and recognised Marguerite's four imprints next to where he had fallen down in the snow. He smiled a natural smile.

It was a busy afternoon. Not too busy, just busy

enough for there to be enough creatures on the streets that it didn't seem like a ghost town but not enough to be stressful. It was a good day for easy banter and polite conversation. Nothing too dark, nothing too secretive. He sidestepped a massive ape in his path.

"Have you ever been to this market?"

"I haven't, actually."

Marguerite gently slapped her hoof against his leg. He felt the pressure of her hoof on his muscles, but nothing more.

"You're missing out. This is the best part of living inside the City."

Before Helmut could answer, they reached the square. Hundreds and hundreds of creatures looked like a slow bee swarm moving across the space. The quiet, yet intense sound of bustling creatures reached Helmut's ear quickly and stuck with him while they entered the chaos. He smelled a thousand flavours coming from all directions.

Spicy curry. Sweet pastries. Hot meat.

Pepper. Salt. Coriander.

Fresh Bread. Apples. Potatoes.

Fried. Grilled. Cooked.

Thyme. Cayenne. Sage.

Rice.

Before his systems could overload, he quickly activated a filter and the overwhelming impressions disappeared behind a shadowy curtain. He was still aware of everything around him, but he didn't experience it as if he was all over the square at once anymore. Helmut sighed, relieved. From somewhere he recognised the distinct sound of old Irish country music being played live.

"Don't you like it?"

Curious. Incipient disappointment.

"I love it. It was just a lot to take in."

Marguerite laughed and stepped closer to him.

"I felt the same when I first came here. So many different things to discover. Come on."

She gently grabbed hold of him and moved purposefully towards the centre. Helmut followed her, enjoying his loss of agency over the situation. It seemed to be an all too familiar pattern in his life, but in this instance, he appreciated it.

"Do I even dare ask where we're headed?"

"It's a surprise, my dear."

Excited voice.

"It's so vast. How have I never been here before?", he wondered out loud.

Marguerite slightly tilted her head, mimicking an all too familiar gesture.

He laughed.

"Stop copying my puzzled look."

"But I always wanted it to be mine. You always look

like you're looking right into someone's soul when you tilt your head like that."

"A keen seer then?" Helmut gently teased.

"Here and there. I seem to have a neck for these sorta things. A gift from my mother, no doubt."

"I barely noticed," he grinned.

Two passing donkeys startled Marguerite.

"Undoubtedly on their way to stalk stallions at the auction."

He laughed a delighted laugh.

"Or maybe they'd like to be auctioned off themselves. It is for charity, after all."

"Who would ever bid on a donkey?"

"I could think of a few creatures who have a secret desire to spend a night with a donkey. I hear great things about their skills…"

"Don't you dare," Marguerite said furiously.

But her eyes gave her away. They told the story of an amused smile instead of anger.

"But then again, I'm generous. As long as you don't feel the need to explore what robots have to offer, you may do as you please."

Helmut hesitated just for a fraction of a second. Marguerite didn't notice.

"Why wouldn't I be with a robot?"

Senses on alert. Analysing.

Marguerite shrugged.

"I'm just messing with you."

Low voice. Deflection.

Wrinkles appeared on Helmut's forehead and he quickly turned his face towards one of the many vendors all around them. He felt the smells, and the sounds and the looks penetrate his shadowy curtain, attempting to get through to him, trying to reach him. A thought crossed his mind.

"Are you hungry?"

"A little," Marguerite admitted.

"How about that grilled salmon over there? I heard it's from the Northern Edges."

The fish sizzled on the grill and small flames rose up when some of its fat touched the charcoal.

"I had fish for dinner yesterday. There's this great stew a few corners from here. You'll love it. Last War Stew."

"Very traditional."

"A girl loves history."

Marguerite stuck her tongue out playfully and turned around.

Helmut had followed Marguerite across the vast square, passing all of the Great Nine creatures. Donkeys and horses had gathered in the far east corner of the square and the loud shouting and laughing of the charity auction spread across the four corners. Eagles foretold fortunes in their corner, their eyes old and wise. Cows and bulls offered pastries and other baked delicacies, foxes stood by the grills where the hunted meat of non-Paradise animals smelled deliciously. Cats and dogs argued in a civil matter about the prices of shiny things, humans and robots engaged in battles of wits over chess and other board games.

And finally, there were the apes. Their stands were in the middle of the square and the snow around them had long since melted if it had ever fallen around their stands. A huge blacksmith's fire stood tall in the middle of them, accessible from eight different directions. The apes working with the fire had shaved their fur off and looked oddly hairless against the bright glow of the fire. Sweat dripped off their bodies, highlighting their thick muscles.

For a short moment, Helmut felt jealousy flicker up from somewhere in his mind, but it disappeared as soon as it had come when he saw Marguerite's glowing eyes.

"This isn't food."

"No, it's not. But I couldn't wait. I have a surprise for you."

Helmut lifted an eyebrow inquiringly.

"You didn't have to…"

"That's the nature of surprises. Of course, I didn't have to. But I wanted to."

"But I don't have anything for you."

"That's the nature of surprises too, little dumb dumb", Marguerite smiled.

"Oh, is that my nickname now?"

"Yes, but only I get to use it."

"I like that," Helmut admitted.

"Now, for the actual surprise. It's a bit out there."

"Some might say that I'm a bit out there as well."

"You are," she grinned. "But once one gets to know you a little better, there's actually a little softy behind that sarcastic, stoic front."

Helmut tilted his head slightly and grinned back silently.

"And what do you want to surprise this little softy with?"

Marguerite tapped one of the apes on his shoulder.

"Marguerite," a high-pitched voice exclaimed.

Recalculating. Female ape.

"Hello, Chrissi. Is my surprise ready?"

"It is indeed, my dear friend. I'll fetch it. You wouldn't believe what happened with James again."

"Oh no, love. Are you still with him?"

"I'll tell you all about it over coffee tomorrow."

"Can't wait."

Chrissi quickly nodded towards Helmut, then disappeared in the workshop.

"You have fascinating friends."

"Surprisingly, you're not the oddest," Marguerite

laughed out loud.

"That's disappointing."

"Be that as it may. I hope that I'll be your oddest with this one. Do you remember the very first time we met?"

"How couldn't I?", Helmut exhaled as if it was just yesterday.

"The way you danced towards me. It reminded me of something. You didn't move like a dancer."

"I will have you know that I dance very well."

"You do," she said gently. "But you're not a dancer. You moved like an ancient warrior. I watched all the movies. You moved through the red shades as if they were blades, as if they would cut you if they touched you. But they didn't touch you, didn't even come close. You were so in rhythm with them and the music."

"I didn't notice."

"Of course, you didn't, my little dumb dumb. But I did. I couldn't help but notice. I had never seen anything like that before."

"Neither had I," Helmut gently whispered.

They shared a look then. Their eyes met. Then, they knew. It was so simple. They didn't need any words to know. To understand. To comprehend.

It was silent then. Sounds couldn't penetrate the bubble that had formed around them. It was just him and her then. A robot and a cow. A cow and a robot. Six legs, two heads, one mind. Helmut and Marguerite.

Chapter Nine

The Mission

It was a quiet day. No sirens had woken Jack from his light sleep which was plagued by despair. No shouting on the streets. Not even Mathena had snored for once, something he was eternally grateful for. But there had been nightmares like there always had been ever since he left his squad behind. Hanna's determined face, Mason's desperate eyes. Ricky's harsh voice, Conny's knowing words. They all had given their lives for him, and what did he do with their sacrifice? Nothing. He got captured and tortured. The intel he had sworn to protect lost to the enemy.

His thoughts were dark that morning when Mathena entered the room. Jack didn't even have breakfast yet, but he eyed a bottle of wine keenly. It had been a long time since he enjoyed some proper wine and he wasn't about to let anything keep him from it.

"What if I told you we could end this war once and for all?"

The cork made a satisfying sound when Jack opened the bottle of red.

"I'd say you're full of crap."

Mathena laughed and shifted slightly on the black

leather couch. Everything in this flat was oddly colourless, almost resembling Jack's black site experience.

"Do you ever not insult everyone and everything around you?"

"No, it's part of my charm. Get used to it."

"Is that how you avoided giving the Donians any intel?"

"Pretty much. I don't know what the fuck is wrong with them, but every time I insulted them, they lost their cool. Stupid clone worshippers."

It hadn't been quite as easy as that, of course. But the lies had come across his lips easier than anything he had ever done before. Easier even than pulling the trigger on enemy soldiers. And damn, if he didn't enjoy putting them down one by one.

"Be that as it may. I have a plan to end this war once and for all with minimal casualties."

"And I still say it's impossible."

Jack poured the wine into two glasses and handed one to Mathena.

"Buddy, I just saved your arse. Show some gratitude."

"Damn, that's some fine shit," Jack exclaimed and took another sip of the wine.

"Where did you get that?"

Mathena sighed. She hadn't given Jack any indication of who she was yet, nor why she saved him, but he didn't care much. She set him free and now he was bound to her. There were worse destinies than that.

Ricky. Mason. Conny. Hanna.

"Paradise's Eagle Scouting Regiment brought it with them the other month. They're the reason, by the way, I was able to find you this quickly."

"Well, I guess I owe Paradise then," Jack laughed delightedly.

"Get it together, Jo. You're a Californian soldier. One of the best we have. I can ill-afford a weak wreck by my side."

Jack's eyes narrowed slightly and a furrow appeared on his forehead.

"Well then. Gimme your fool-proof plan."

"We kill the President."

"We've killed five of the goddamn Don clones already. There's no stopping them."

"13, to be precise. But I don't just mean the current President. We'll kill them all. Once and for all."

"All of them? There's only one President."

"There's more than that. Have you ever thought about how there's always a next clone ready to step in?"

"Not really. I follow orders. I'm not paid to think or strategise," Jack admitted.

"Well, that's about to change, soldier. Welcome to your new life."

Mathena stood up and opened the windows of their

flat. The shy whispering of birds flooded the room. Jack appreciated the gust of fresh air coming with it. All he had breathed in for the past few days was the stifling air of the black site.

"Until recently, we had no idea about how it worked either. It took us a goddamn 100 years to figure it out."

"Will you enlighten me anytime soon or should I get myself another glass of that delicious red wine?"

"There's a school. A school of little clones who are raised, educated and trained by elderly clones. All based on the Don's gene pool. When the President clone dies, the most advanced of them becomes the next one. It's simple but brilliant. They teach each other and provide their knowledge to future generations."

Jack looked thoughtful for a moment. When he spoke, his tongue had turned blue from the wine.

"So, you're suggesting to kill innocent children."

"They're not innocent."

"They haven't committed any crimes yet."

"But they will."

"There'll be others. Other children who won't grow up to be the President. Children who are just there and who won't hurt a soul. The collateral damage will be immense. Massive. How can you suggest something like that?"

There wasn't a lot Jack wouldn't do to win this war. He had been fighting for years, but all he had to show for it was a myriad of dead soldiers and friends alike. He'd give anything to win, but killing innocent children was something too dark even for him. Even if one of them might grow up to become the next President.

"They are the enemy, regardless. We must kill them. For the greater good of our citizens, and theirs, I might add. Kill them, and the war is over. They're the past, the present and the future in one. We eliminate them, we eliminate the last bit of the North American Empire once and for all."

Jack stood up and walked to the window. Little children played in the park, adults walked across the streets, drank coffee and talked as if there was no war at all. He had left behind the life of a civilian a long time ago to serve his state. It looked oddly similar to the life of his people in California. Unknowing, unquestioning, undaring.

"There'll be back-ups. Secret schools. Gene material we won't be able to destroy."

What Mathena proposed made sense. Too much sense to simply ignore it, despite his moral objections. He had to entertain the idea, as much as he hated the thought of killing innocent lives, even if they were tomorrow's danger. He had sworn an oath to serve and protect the Independent State of California. He wasn't about to back down from that, not after everything he had been through.

“No, there’s only this one school. We have feasible intel on it.”

“Even if that were true, what about the gene material? They’d just clone another one.”

“They might, but cloning takes time. It’s a dangerous process even after all this time. Their technology isn’t what Paradise’s used to be, even before they banned further experiments.”

“They’ll still manage to clone another one.”

“So be it. But he’ll be lacking a crucial thing: guidance by his former clones. He’ll be alone in the world. Nobody guides him. Nobody teaches him. Nobody leads him. California can take a single clone.”

“Is there no better idea than that? It’ll be a suicide mission.”

“Your fellow soldiers have died for our cause. Your friends have died for it. So has your family. Why not you as well?”

Mathena stared into Jack’s eyes, right into him. He tried to escape her gaze, but couldn’t. Cold shivers ran down his back.

“You want to kill children?”

He knew that his objection sounded weak. Their enemies wouldn’t hesitate for a second if such a chance presented itself to them.

“I’ll do what I must to guarantee my people’s survival.”

"And there's no other way? None at all?"

"We've tried everything, Jo. For the past 100 years, we've tried everything, and yet the war is raging on. If all I have to do is to kill children who'll grow up to be monsters anyway, I'll do it while singing them a lullaby."

She finished her glass and grabbed the bottle to pour herself another. There wasn't much left.

"It still seems wrong. You wouldn't ask me to simply kill civilians. We've never done that. We pride ourselves on being different from them."

He too poured himself another glass and chucked it down immediately. The bitter taste in his mouth made him frown for a moment, then the alcohol entered his bloodstream.

"Damn, that's some strong stuff."

Mathena circled the red liquid in her glass and watched its movement for a long second.

"If we kill them now, think about how many lives we'll save. You're not the only one to have lost your loved ones in this conflict, Jack. I'll kill anyone in my way to achieve peace. And if I have to walk over a few dead children, innocent or not, I will. They're not the future. We are."

"And this is sanctioned by Central Command?"

"Central Command trusts me enough to operate freely behind enemy lines. Why do you think they sent me to free you? We have it in our hands. This is us now."

Jack remained silent, but Mathena felt that she was close to a breakthrough.

"You won't have to kill them, Jo. I will. All I need from you is to help me get there. If we had done that a few weeks earlier, Mason and Ricky, Hanna and Conny would still be alive. How much would you give to bring them back?"

Jack hesitated. Their faces flashed in front of his eyes. Their stories. Their families. Their hopes and dreams. Their plans for after the war. What they would have done to save him, their sacrifice to aid his escape and how he had let them down. Every single one of them. At that moment, he realised he'd do anything for them. Anything.

"What do you need me to do?"

Chapter Ten

The Fellowship

"I read your report, Helmut. Very sophisticated."

"Thank you, Councillor."

A shy smile appeared on Helmut's lips.

"Which of you came up with that plan?"

"All the credit should go to Susan. She's the creative one of us."

Councillor Christine's eyes switched over to Susan.

"And here I thought you were nothing but a leak to the First Councillor."

"Your trust in me honours you, Madame."

Sarcastic. Dangerous.

But Councillor Christine seemed to be in a good mood.

"I guess I deserve that. Tell me then. How did you come up with it?"

"It's all in the report, Madame."

"I know. But I'd like to hear it from you. It's not every day that we get one over the foxes, let alone their Ambassador. My people have a particular distaste for them."

Her words hung portentous in the air.

"Well, Madame, Helmut and I had a hunch that the Fox Ambassador would know more than he would tell us either way. We just didn't know how much. We had reason to assume that the killed fox was involved in some sort of clandestine operation in the City, though we can only speculate as to its reasoning or success."

"Yes, I was wondering about that. How did you come to that conclusion?"

"We had heard rumours from our Agency sources on the ground," Helmut interjected. "There was reason to believe that the dead fox was part of something larger and the later autopsy of the body confirmed that. It had tattoos on its body which are akin to special operations."

The lies left his lips easier than he had anticipated. It was a dangerous game they were playing, but given that they still didn't know what role the Councillor played in all of this, they had decided to withhold the information the Californian Ambassador had given them. Rather, they neglected to tell their involvement with a friendly, yet foreign power.

Scanning. No signs of mistrust detected.

"So, you came up with this little trick to see whether the Fox Ambassador was truthful."

"Indeed, Madame. Once we realised that the dead fox was part of something larger, we had to know how deep it ran. So, instead of bringing him the actual DNA of the killed fox, we used some from the archives. An old case, in fact. Years ago. We mixed the DNA with a self-destroying substance which would make a later analysis of the sample impossible. When we were in the Ambassador's office, Helmut checked their machinery. We found that the model they employed wasn't able to save the data for a second analysis. That was our green light. It worked."

"Very smart," the Councillor nodded. "Though dangerous."

"Be that as it may. Once the Ambassador provided us with the identity which didn't match the one we had provided him with, we knew that they had manipulated the machinery beforehand. So regardless of what sample we'd given them, we would have received the information they wanted us to receive."

"Ah yes, the infamous Kristian Dioti. He does exist, you know."

"It wouldn't make much sense if he hadn't existed. I wonder how they disappeared him."

"We're not yet certain whether they actually killed him."

Helmut narrowed his eyes and focused on the Councillor.

"Excuse me?"

"Once I read your report, I checked in with the Agency. They confirmed that his troupe left a day after the murder. One fox down, but their baggage was slightly heavier than before. Exactly what an average fox would weigh. We assume they smuggled Dioti out of Paradise and back into Fox Nation."

"That's a great risk," Susan said.

"It is," Councillor Christine nodded.

"Unless he is of some use to them."

"I arrived at the same conclusion."

"Are we certain he's alive? Do we know anything else about him?"

"Only what's in the public records. So not too much. We don't yet know how, or even if, he's involved. But it would appear that he's your only lead at this stage, am I correct?"

"Not necessarily, Madame. We do know that the Fox Ambassador, and thus, Fox Nation was at least aware of their special operative and that they're trying to shield his identity from us."

Councillor Christine nodded to herself and seemed to think for a moment.

"Is there reason to believe that the dead fox is involved in the original murder of the bull?"

"No, it was the Centaur all along," Helmut almost caught himself saying.

But he didn't. Of course, he didn't. He had no proof of the Centaur's existence, nor that this mythical creature somehow undetectably murdered two of Paradise's citizens.

"Truth be told, Councillor, we don't know who killed the bull yet."

"Do you have any leads?"

You.

"Nothing feasible as of yet. We still believe the carvings to have some sort of meaning but nothing in particular that we could point towards at this stage in our investigation."

"I'll ask again then. Do you believe that the fox was involved in the murder of the bull?"

Impatient.

"Yes."

Susan's voice cut through the air like a blade. Helmut turned around to Susan, utterly surprised. But her eyes backed him to trust her.

Speechless. Restart riposte folder.

And so, he did.

"Well, then. Say your goodbyes to this place. You're going on an adventure."

Riposte folder restarted.

"And here I thought all of this was my adventure," Helmut replied dryly.

Susan giggled quietly.

The cow gave both of them a dark stare.

"This is serious."

"Of course, Councillor."

"Absolutely, Madame."

"I need your full attention."

There was something in her voice that startled Susan and she stopped her banter immediately. Helmut's dark eyes focused on the cow, who glared at the two investigators. One of her four legs angrily hit the floor.

"Now listen up. You're going to Fox Nation. Congratulations."

Helmut shook the snow off his coat and entered the old coffee house. It was too early to head to the bar, and thus, he and Susan needed a new place to conspire. They had chosen a cosy place with an open fire in the taproom.

"What can I get the two of you?"

The waitress smiled a welcome.

"Just some hot chocolate for me," Susan whispered.

"Make that two. With two extra shots of whiskey, please."

"Of course. Will that be all?"

Susan hesitated.

"Do you have any cake today?"

"Absolutely. In fact, the cheesecake is just coming out of the oven."

The waitress leaned towards Susan and her face disappeared behind a dark curtain of hair. Her pointed ears stood upright in the air.

"It's quite delicious. I sneaked a piece away for

myself earlier. Delicious indeed."

"We'll have two then, with extra whipped cream, please."

The cat nodded and moved towards the kitchen. Her tail swung wildly in the air.

Positive mood.

There was a silence then when Helmut and Susan both looked utterly thoughtful and oddly content with their situation.

"So, do you care to tell me what that was all about?"

Though his voice was calm, his displeasure with the recent turn of events was palpable.

"I had an idea. We don't have any feasible leads for the Fallen Bull case. None whatsoever. Even our theory regarding the carvings seems to have evaporated into thin air. There's nothing there for us right now. Too many uncertain variables and a Cow Councillor who clearly tries to interfere in our investigation. That drug-test was at minimum a warning, probably an attempt to get us, or at least me, thrown off the case."

"We agree on that then. But why did you tell the Councillor that we believe there's a connection? Now we have to go to Fox Nation, for fucks sake."

"She was obviously looking for an excuse to send us away. That, in itself, says more than anything else in this investigation so far."

Helmut thought for a moment, then nodded.

"She did seem to be particularly focused on the connection between the two murders."

"So, I figured I'd give her what she desires before she excludes us from the investigation altogether. We haven't been particularly successful so far."

"Fair point."

"But there's something else. Our only current lead is the Fox Ambassador and his shady dealings. But he's got to get his orders from somewhere. And, more importantly, either Dioti is still alive, or the foxes smuggled something else out of continental Paradise. Something as heavy as an average fox. It might as well be whatever the fox stole from the Californians. Besides, the Californian Ambassador mentioned her operatives clashed with the Centaur's organisation in the City of Spies. Maybe we can kill two birds with one stone."

"That's a wild guess. Why would they execute their own operative for that?"

"It's just a wild guess. But regardless, we have better chances to find the reason for the clandestine operation in Fox Nation than here. Maybe with that information, this whole mess will finally resolve itself."

"Somehow, I doubt that."

"And somehow I doubt that the first-ever murder in Paradise, the appearance of a fox operative just days after the murder, a suspicious Cow Councillor and the involvement of California are all unconnected."

Before Helmut could answer, the cat waitress returned, almost floating above the smooth and shiny surface.

"There we are," she snorted.

She placed two steaming cups of hot chocolate in front of Helmut and Susan, followed by two plates of delicious-looking cheesecake, whipped cream majestically mounted on top of the cake. Helmut smelled the whiskey in the cups.

Sweet relief incoming. Relax.

Chapter Eleven

Goodbyes

The next few days passed by on the fly. There wasn't much for Helmut to do and yet, it felt as if it all happened just a bit too rapidly. He said goodbye to his favourite places, returned to the two crime scenes with the City's square being his favourite, and ultimately ended his little farewell where he began his journey in the first place: the bar.

"I can't believe you're leaving tomorrow."

Neshama poured him yet another drink, his third of the night.

"Me neither. But it won't be for long."

"Men always say that and then they never return."

Bitter voice despite the intended joke.

"I'm no mere man."

"That's what they all say," she laughed.

This time, it was an honest one.

If only I could tell you guys the truth.

"Well then, I guess I'm just your average lying man just as you know us to be."

"That's how I like them best," she grinned.

"Lucky me."

He gave her a smile and got up. A sword was tied to

his back, its weight oddly reassuring.

"I didn't know you were carrying that thing with you."

"Me neither, but when I packed my bags today, I figured it might be useful."

"You are travelling to Sig's Canal, so who knows what shenanigans you'll experience there."

This lie hadn't come as easy as the ones they had told the Fox Ambassador and the Cow Councillor, but it was necessary. He and Susan had decided that they couldn't share their destination with anyone, not even Neshama or Marguerite. The words had felt bitter when he spoke them, but ultimately he knew it was better and safer for all of them this way.

"Are you sure that's the only reason you're taking it with you, though?"

Neshama's voice pulled him out of his train of thought.

He smiled.

"It's her gift. I'll always carry it close to my heart."

"You speak of her as if she's dead."

"She's very much alive," Helmut laughed.

"Oh, I know. Our kitchen is a mess right now. She's attempting to bake cookies. Again. Cow hooves and baking just isn't a good match, but she refuses to accept defeat just yet."

"Luckily, us humans have been gifted with hands and thumbs."

Helmut winked at Neshama.

"That's just life, I guess."

"Anyway. I should get going. Early morning and all that."

"Like you've ever cared about that."

He smirked then.

"Well, one more won't hurt."

Neshama rolled her eyes and poured him another oddly green drink.

The next morning, Helmut met Susan at the airfield. It was a snowy day, as it had always been lately. He recognised the Councillor's light imprints in the snow.

"Still carrying that with you, then?"

Helmut took the sword off his back and held it in his hand. It was lighter than he had anticipated when Marguerite handed it to him on the market square.

"I figured I might want to duel a fox when we're in Fox Nation."

"You'd undoubtedly lose."

"I would, but then you could finally be useful and attend my wounds."

"I'd let you bleed out right there and then. You've been nothing but a pain in my arse."

"Oh, you wish I was a pain in your arse."

With a swift motion, Helmut moved the blade through the air. His exceptional eyesight recognised how the thin blade cut through the tiny snowflakes all around them.

"Are you ready?"

Helmut and Susan immediately saluted at the sound of the Councillor's voice.

"Yes, Madame."

"Of course, Councillor Christine."

"Excellent. Follow me then."

She turned around and headed in the opposite direction from the huge transport plane standing ready. Helmut and Susan shared a look.

"Madame, where are we headed?"

"Your train, of course."

"Our train, Councillor?"

"Yes, your train. That plane here is going towards the Canal. You're going to the Capital of Spies. Nobody is going to suspect you're coming via train."

"But it'll take days to reach Fox Nation that way."

"A few days won't hurt. Besides, this way, everyone thinks you're going to the Canal, just as we want them to think."

It made sense. It'd be too odd if there was no actual proof that they headed towards the Canal.

After a few minutes, they reached the underground station.

"Nobody knows about this station. It's an old memory of the Last War. This was meant to be the Capital's escape route once upon a time. Fortunately, nobody ever needed to use it and so nobody knows about it today. But now it'll do us good. I pray each day we never have to rely on it again."

"Of course, Madame."

"Now, I know this is a bit sudden, but the Council hopes that you'll find out how Fox Nation is connected to all of this. Tread carefully over there. While it's still Paradise, the rules are different there. Their autonomy has made them brisk and arrogant. One of the Agency's agents will welcome you to the Capital of Spies. You're envoys on a civil mission. If you blow your cover, we'll get you back here."

"Thank you, Councillor. We'll be in touch."

The train began to move without making any sounds. Helmut sat by the window, watching the City fly past him. Despite the snow, the railways were clear. He leaned back and closed his eyes. Finally, some peace. It'd be a long journey and only a small part of that would be in a private carriage. Soon enough, there'd be hundreds of other creatures around them. Some on their way to friends and family, others on vacation and yet others on business. It'd be crowded and loud. Though he didn't need to sleep, he did enjoy the feeling of it. Just a few hours before he'd have to be awake again.

"Has it a name yet?"

But of course, Susan was well-awake.

"What?"

He opened his eyes and inspected Susan.

"Your sword. Does it have a name yet?"

"Yes."

"Oh come on. Don't make me squeeze it out of you little by little."

"Why do you want to know?"

"One day, you might defend my honour with it. I'd like to know who to thank then."

He grinned at her invitation.

"Syphilis. You can thank Syphilis for defending your honour then."

And when he spoke its name, his eyes were dark and sharp and utterly green.

Epilogue

The Finalisation

It could be a historical day, or the end of it all. The sun was just rising over Paradise. It promised to be a beautiful summer morning in the City. The air was just right, still fresh and unconsumed, not too stifling and hot yet. Christine took a deep breath. She felt free then, maybe for the last time in a long while. She didn't know what the future would hold for her after today. This was the day she had been working towards for so long. That they had been working towards. Corps stood right next to her on a mountain just outside the City's outskirts. Just far enough from the City to escape its sounds, its citizens, its troubles and intrigues. Just far enough from the City so that nobody would suspect a secret meeting here.

Corps sighed and stretched his arms, almost as if he wanted to hug the City. Then he flashed a cheeky, almost childish smile.

"Everything is in place. The Combrines are in their hangar in the City, waiting to be released. The computer drawing the next Cow Councillor has been infiltrated and will almost certainly produce you as the next Councillor."

“Almost certainly?”

“You know how it is. Code sometimes takes on a life of its own.”

Christine stared at him. Had she placed her future into the hands of a lunatic?

“I’m just messing with you. It’s foolproof.”

“You haven’t changed one bit.”

“Why would I? Speaking of the Councillor. She’ll have a devastating heart attack later. So sad. She was actually one of the good ones for Paradise. It’s a pity she had to stand in the way of progress.”

“Pity? I didn’t know you of all people would be sentimental about this.”

“I’m not,” he chuckled, but his eyes were dark and cold.

Christine mirrored his grin. Slowly her excitement overtook her anxiety. She took a deep breath and exhaled through her lips.

“I’m ready to take her place and promote our plan.”

“Are you ready to rewrite history then?”

“There’s only so many histories to be written.”

“There’s only one to be exact. Ours.”

Christine shook her head in amusement.

“Sometimes I wonder whether you’d be a king in another life. You certainly have the arrogance for it.”

“I’m more than a mere king here. I’m a creator. Why be a miserable king when you can be a god? Why depend on people and creatures when you can create your own following, your own people, your own place in history?"

A puff of wind played with Corps' hair and shuffled it around. He ran a hand through his dark beard and smiled. Sunbeams reflected in his whiter than white teeth.

"You are that then to your creations? To the Combrines. You're their god?"

Corps laughed and raised his eyebrows.

"This isn't about my godlikeness, this is about something else entirely or have you forgotten why we have created the Combrines?"

"No, of course not. It's with me every damn day. But I fear you're putting too much hope into this. I always thought gods wouldn't be hopeful."

Beneath them, the City slowly awoke. Eagles began to leave their nests and fly towards the centre, cows and horses galloped through the streets, apes started their morning yoga in the early morning sun, dogs attempted to brew coffee and cats opened their breakfast cafes. Foxes crawled out of their holes in the ground, donkeys opened their first bottles of beer, and humans sleepily opened their eyes in comfortable beds. And then, there were the robots, who unplugged from their charging stations and received their coding instructions from the Council's tower. Christine stood tall at the edge of the mountain, a tear running down her cheek.

Paradise's citizens existed in peace then, and regardless of what the future would hold for her, Christine swore herself in that moment to always protect Paradise, no matter what. Even if that meant committing necessary evils as she had done when she accepted Corps' proposal.

"My entire empire has been built on hope. I live to hope. What else is there when all else has failed? The Combrines are my last hope. I am their Master by design, but they've been built and coded to act independently from me or anyone, really."

"So, they could turn against you then? Hypothetically speaking, of course."

"Hypothetically speaking, everyone can turn on everyone. Of course, we are the exception."

He rolled his eyes playfully and continued.

"But if that should ever happen, I have created a failsafe, so to speak."

"Smart. Good call. What is it?"

"Not every secret is meant for you, my dear Christine."

Christine sighed. She knew when she was being played. But Corps surprised her on this sunny morning.

"I have created three sets of markings which will grant you total control over the Combrines. They have to be exposed to all three of them, but not at once. If they see all three at once, their entire systems break down and they die and destroy themselves. However, if they see the markings separated by a certain period of time, it will gradually grant you more control over them without anybody ever noticing."

"What are the three stages?"

"The first will ensure that the Combrines won't attempt to hurt you or conspire against you. There's a free space in the first carving where you can include your name as a rune so that they know who not to hurt. However, they're not aware that they're being manipulated that way, obviously."

"That sounds complicated."

"Complicated doesn't even begin to describe it. It's my greatest achievement yet."

"You're that proud of your creations?"

Corps didn't say a word, but his eyes sparkled in pride and satisfaction.

"The second carving will ensure that they protect you against all threats, internal and external alike, again, without them even knowing about it. As they're created to act autonomously, it'd run against their code and entire being if they knew they'd be manipulated that way."

"So, the carvings make them my slaves then, in a way."

"All robots are slaves, they just don't know it yet.

Well, except mine, of course."

"Of course. You sound like a proud daddy sending his daughter off to Prom."

Corps laughed an unusually loud laugh and startled a few nearby birds who idly sat in the trees around them.

"And then there's the third carving, the ultimate finisher. Once the Combrines have been exposed to it, all their moral compasses and codes are overwritten. Their only purpose, then, is to serve you. There's nothing that can stop that process then. Even shutting them down and entirely resetting them couldn't overwrite that. They're your ultimate servants then. The only way to stop them following your every order is to expose them to all three carvings or entirely killing and destroying every bit of them. A task so monumental, it'd be almost impossible."

Christine gasped in astonishment before a frown covered her face momentarily.

"Why not just start with that? Isn't that their purpose?"

"No!"

Corps' words were sharp and cold. His eyes furious and angry. His mouth a thin line of disappointment.

"No, you haven't listened carefully then. They're designed to act autonomously, interact with all other creatures, survive without being detected. That last step would make that impossible, render the beauty of the Combrines to nothing, reduce them to mere animals."

"So, basically, turn them into regular first-gen robots."

He took a deep breath and seemed to calm down.

"I understand why you'd arrive at that conclusion, but that's not the purpose they were designed for. It's a failsafe. That last one should only be introduced in desperate times when all else has failed. They will be murderous terminators with that command. They're scary enough already, do not believe for a second that I'd ever want them to turn into that third stage."

"Why then create such a code at all?"

"If Paradise is ever threatened again and I'm not around anymore, that third step will grant someone all power over the Combrines to defend Paradise against whatever comes for it. Whatever happens, Paradise must survive. We're the last bastion, we're the ones to have survived death, we're nature's audacity."

"We are indeed. But why then have the feature where they're shut off entirely if exposed to all three of them at the same time? That would be a major weakness if it ever came to the survival of Paradise."

"I believe all creatures can be corrupted. Even the Combrines, for all their flawlessness. If there should ever be the need, and I'm not around, I want someone to have the power to turn them off."

Christine's eyes widened in recognition.

"And you want me to be the one?"

Corps smiled.

"One of them. One of three, to be exact. That way, even if one or two of my chosen Guardians should betray me, go missing or die, there's still one to take control."

Corps opened his backpack and handed Christine a flash drive and a dark envelope.

"Here, one is a digital file, one is a physical picture. Store them well, store them safely. Rise now, Guardian of the Combrines, Cow Councillor Christine, my trusted friend and Protector of Paradise."

The End

To be continued...

Printed in Great Britain
by Amazon

68033816R00135